"I don't want you to be afraid of me, Pippa," Nick said, his voice low.

He gazed into her green eyes. "Not ever. If I do anything that frightens you, tell me and I'll stop, I promise." His thumb reached up to feather across her lips. "See? I'm harmless. I don't have . . ." He lowered his head toward hers. ". . . a threatening bone in my body."

Was he crazy? Pippa's mind yelled. He was threatening to the entire female population just by breathing. He was . . . Oh, my. Oh . . . yes.

As Nick's lips covered hers, all rational thought fled. His hand was cradling her cheek, his body was barely touching hers, but she was on fire with need. It wasn't fear anymore that made her tremble. It was passion. . . .

WHAT ARE *LOVESWEPT* ROMANCES?

They are stories of true romance and touching emotion. We believe those two very important ingredients are constants in our highly sensual and very believable stories in the *LOVESWEPT* line. Our goal is to give you, the reader, stories of consistently high quality that may sometimes make you laugh, sometimes make you cry, but are always fresh and creative and contain many delightful surprises within their pages.

Most romance fans read an enormous number of books. Those they truly love, they keep. Others may be traded with friends and soon forgotten. We hope that each *LOVESWEPT* romance will be a treasure—a "keeper." We will always try to publish

LOVE STORIES YOU'LL NEVER FORGET
BY AUTHORS YOU'LL ALWAYS REMEMBER

The Editors

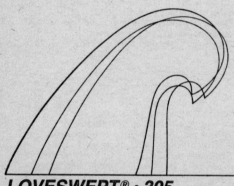

LOVESWEPT® · 305

Joan Elliott Pickart
Serenity Cove

 BANTAM BOOKS
TORONTO · NEW YORK · LONDON · SYDNEY · AUCKLAND

SERENITY COVE

A Bantam Book / January 1989

*LOVESWEPT® and the wave device are registered
trademarks of Bantam Books, a division of
Bantam Doubleday Dell Publishing Group, Inc.
Registered in U.S. Patent
and Trademark Office and elsewhere.*

*If you would be interested in receiving protective vinyl
covers for your Loveswept books, please write to this address
for information:*

> *Loveswept
> Bantam Books
> P.O. Box 985
> Hicksville, NY 11802*

ISBN 0-553-21960-X

Published simultaneously in the United States and Canada

---

*Bantam Books are published by Bantam Books, a division
of Bantam Doubleday Dell Publishing Group, Inc. Its trademark, consisting of the words "Bantam Books" and the
portrayal of a rooster, is Registered in U.S. Patent and
Trademark Office and in other countries. Marca Registrada.
Bantam Books, 666 Fifth Avenue, New York, New York 10103.*

PRINTED IN THE UNITED STATES OF AMERICA

O   0 9 8 7 6 5 4 3 2 1

For the 3750th Security Police
Squadron/"C" Flight,
Sheppard Air Force Base.
Sincerest thanks to you all
for taking such good care
of that special one among you,
my daughter, Airman Tracey Pickart.

One

Nick Capoletti arrived at the cabin at 1:17 A.M.

He let himself in with the key his travel agent had given him, stumbled across the moonlit room, and collapsed onto the sofa.

He had never been so exhausted in his entire life. He should have stopped hours before at a motel and driven on to the cabin in the morning, rested, refreshed, and raring to go. Well, what was done was done. He was there.

Somewhere in the place, he supposed, was a bedroom with a bed, but at the moment he didn't care. All he wanted was to sleep, and the sofa would do just fine.

He tugged off his shoes and jeans, decided his T-shirt could stay on, and stretched out on the sofa with a weary sigh.

At 1:27 A.M., Nick was deeply asleep.

At 1:36 A.M., he rolled over and with absolutely no style or grace fell off the sofa and landed on the floor with a resounding thud.

He muttered a curse in Italian, then smacked his hand along the sofa until he connected with a throw pillow. He yanked it off, stuffed it under his head, and closed his eyes.

At 1:39 A.M., he was asleep again.

At 9:12 the next morning, an annoying and strange noise penetrated Nick's haze of sleep, nudging against his brain and forcing him to surface to consciousness.

The noise, he realized groggily, was someone clearing his throat in a manner that indicated displeasure and demanded attention.

He groaned, opened his eyes halfway, and found himself looking at a pair of slender, bare, feminine feet. Said feet had toenails painted the color of ripe watermelon. Said feet were tanned and quite attractive, as far as feet went. And one of the said feet was tapping in a steady rhythm that virtually shouted impatience.

Fascinating, Nick mused, still not totally awake. It was nice of the feet to drop by, but where was he? Oh, yeah. It was coming to him now. The cabin, his bone-crushing fatigue, the sofa, and . . . Oh, yeah, the floor.

He was, it would seem, lying on his stomach, clad in an orange T-shirt and royal-blue Jockey shorts, his head on a lace-edged throw pillow, and watching a one-footed tap dance by a slender foot with watermelon-colored toes. Fascinating.

He shifted his head upward, scrutinizing the trim ankles attached to the feet, then the shapely, lightly tanned legs. Above them pink shorts fit enticingly over a woman's hips. Deciding the rewards of his perusal were dandy so far, he kept going. A pink-and-white-striped cotton blouse was next, covering firm, rounded breasts. A lovely neck. Now for the face.

Oh, say, Nick thought, his eyes definitely fully opened, if it weren't for the crabby expression, that would be one beautiful face.

Framed by a wild tumble of shoulder-length black hair, the face had delicate features, a pert nose with a dusting of freckles, luscious lips, and the greenest eyes he'd ever seen.

Nick's photographic memory clicked a picture of the entire woman and delivered it to his brain. She was definitely nice to wake up to, he thought. Trim, small-boned, and delicate, probably about twenty-five, and quite lovely in a wholesome, no-frills way. She was, however, still tapping that foot and clearing her throat, and her expression indicated she was none too happy. So, what was her problem?

"Hi," he said, flashing her a smile. "What's your problem?"

Problem? Pippa thought. Her problem was trying to concentrate on staying irritated when her heart was beating like a bongo drum. She was not in the habit of discovering half-naked men sleeping on the floor of one of her cabins. Especially a man like that one. With long, muscular legs; broad shoulders; a knock-out smile on a face so handsome her breath caught in her throat; thick, tousled black hair; dark eyes; and the nicest buns she'd ever seen, this man was incredible. This man was also not supposed to be there.

"You're not supposed to be here," she said, staring down at him.

"Sure, I am. I have a reservation."

"You were due sometime this afternoon."

"Oh, that." He folded his arms under his head. "Well, I drove straight through and got in last night. I started out on the sofa, but fell off. I think I broke my body."

Heaven forbid, Pippa thought. That body should be pampered, caressed by the soft hands of a woman. *Her* hands. Oh, for Pete's sake, how ridiculous.

"I assume," she said stiffly, "that you're Mr. Capoletti?"

"In the flesh," he said cheerfully. He glanced over his shoulder at his partially clad body. "Almost literally. Who are you?"

"Mrs. Pippa Pauling, the manager of this establishment. And, please, no remarks about my name. I've heard them all."

He yawned. "It's a great name, cute as a button. I like it." His eyes drifted closed.

"Hey," she said, "you can't go back to sleep. I have to get this cabin ready for your arrival." Why did that sound dumb? "Mr. Capoletti?"

"That's dumb," he mumbled. "I'm already here. Oh, and it's Nick. Call me Nick, I'll call you Pippa. Pippa Pauling. That's really very cute. 'Bye."

"Mr. . . . Nick. I have things that must be done in this cabin."

"Work around me. I'm really bushed," he said, not opening his eyes.

"You're disrupting my schedule. Besides, didn't it occur to you that other people might still be in here? You would have frightened them terribly." She leaned over and peered closely at him. "Hello? Well, great, he's asleep."

The front door burst open and a little girl ran in, dark braids flying. "I finished my breakfast, Mommy," she said. "Grandpa says I can go to town with him. 'Kay?" She stopped abruptly and stared wide-eyed at Nick. "Oh, a dead body. A dead, dead body, just like in the movie I watched at Beth Ann's, 'cept the body in the movie was all bloody and yucky."

"Emma, I'm really going to have to speak with Beth Ann's mother about the videos she rents when you spend the night. Mr. Capoletti is not dead. He's asleep."

"*Was* asleep," Nick said gruffly, lifting his head. He blinked at the little girl. "A miniature Pippa. Same eyes, freckles, the whole bit."

"I'm Emma," she said. "Why are you sleeping on the floor?"

"It just ended up that way."

"Oh. I have blue undies, too, only mine gots lace on them. What's your name, besides Mr. Capoletti?"

"Nick."

"Emma," Pippa said, "you go on with Grandpa. Nick isn't exactly dressed for visitors."

"*You're* visiting Nick, Mommy. How come *you* get to visit Nick when he's in his undies?"

"Yeah," Nick said, grinning up at Pippa, "how come?"

Pippa glared at Nick, then looked at Emma again. "Don't keep Grandpa waiting, sweetheart. He has the shopping list that Grandma and I made up, and you can be his helper."

"Next week when I have my birthday and I'm six," Emma said, "I'll be a bigger helper."

Pippa smiled. "You certainly will."

Emma ran toward the door. " 'Bye, Mommy. 'Bye, Nick. I'll tell Grandpa you're visiting Nick in his undies, Mommy. He said you were cleaning over here. 'Bye."

"Emma!" Pippa called after her. "Don't say that I'm—Oh, good grief."

Nick chuckled. " '—visiting Nick in his undies.' Interesting thought. Well, good night." He lowered his head and closed his eyes. An instant later his head popped up again. "Hey, whoa. Is your husband going to hear the news flash about you, me, and my undies when Grandpa does?"

"I don't have a husband."

"Oh. Well, does Grandpa tote a shotgun, or anything?"

"No, of course not."

"Good." He plopped his head back onto the pillow.

"All right, fine," Pippa said, throwing up her hands. "I'll work around you, but don't blame me if the noise disturbs you. I have to stay on schedule. I really didn't expect you until this afternoon, you know."

"Feel free to dust me," he mumbled, "but I draw the line at being vacuumed."

She shook her head and started away, only to stop and allow her gaze to slide over Nick's body once again.

He really was magnificent, she mused. His legs looked so powerful and were covered by dark curly hair. He probably had dark curly hair on his chest, too. Dust him? Every delicious inch? Wouldn't that be a delightful experience?

Pippa Pauling, stop it! Where on earth were those bizarre thoughts coming from? She never gawked at or fantasized about the guests at Serenity Cove. But in all fairness to herself, she'd never had a guest quite like Nick Capoletti before. Or at least not one who'd arrived without a woman.

She continued to stare at Nick, and was suddenly aware of heat throbbing deep within her. How would it feel, she wondered, to be held in those strong arms, pressed to that hard body? What would it be like to make love with a man like Nick? It had been so long, so very long, since . . . Enough. She wasn't behaving like herself at all, and her wanton mental ramblings were putting her terribly behind schedule. She spun around and marched out of the living room.

Nick cautiously opened one eye and watched Pippa leave the room. He closed his eye again and sighed with relief.

Thank goodness she was gone, he thought. And thank goodness the entire episode had taken place while he'd been lying on his stomach. Pippa Pauling had thrown his libido into overdrive. Every lovely inch of her was stamped indelibly in his mind for him to examine at his leisure. With that picture was the lingering memory of her light floral cologne, which he'd inhaled when she'd bent over him.

Her hair was sensational. Black and silky, wild and wavy, it looked as though she'd spent hours in a hair salon. But he knew her hair was natural, just as all of her was. She was a world apart from the glitzy women he knew in Las Vegas. And the very sight of her had knocked him for a loop.

He chuckled, then glanced up quickly to make sure Pippa hadn't heard him. Resting his head on the pillow again, he recalled what her daughter had said—"visiting Nick in his undies." What a sensual scene that conjured up. He'd better get his thinking back on the straight and narrow, or he'd never be able to get off the floor without embarrassing himself to death. His body was going nuts.

The little girl was a safe topic, he decided. She was a cute kid, and looked so much like Pippa, it was as though the father had had nothing to do with creating her. Speaking of which, what had happened to the absent Mr. Pauling? Divorce, probably. Well, it was Mr. Pauling's loss that he was no longer around to enjoy the lovely Pippa and nifty Emma.

And would Nick Capoletti gain? he wondered. No, it wouldn't happen. He wasn't against vacation flings, but not with someone like Pippa. He sensed she didn't play those kind of games. She was a mother, for crying out loud. But, oh, Lord, she had the most kissable lips he'd ever seen. Her eyes were like emeralds, and her body . . . Yes, her body would nestle perfectly against his, her long legs tangling with his and . . . And if he didn't get his act together, he was going to spend the day on the floor, hiding the evidence of his wayward thoughts.

He lifted his head again, and heard Pippa banging around in the kitchen. His jeans were in a heap on the floor, and he quickly stood and pulled them on. With sunlight pouring in the windows, he finally looked around the cabin.

Paneled in dark wood and decorated with Early American furniture, it had a cozy, welcoming feel. There was a fireplace on one wall, and rag rugs were scattered here and there on the gleaming hardwood floor. It was a fairly large place, more like a small home than his idea of a cabin.

Serenity Cove was, according to the brochure his travel agent had given him, located in an area thick with pine trees. There was a lake for fishing and boating, and a small town fifteen miles down the mountain.

He was definitely on top of a mountain, over a mile above sea level. If he gave much thought to those dark, winding roads he'd maneuvered while half-asleep the night before, he'd probably scare himself to death.

Nick crossed the room and looked out the window. Yes, there were the endless pine trees, lush and green, cool and inviting. It was hard to believe he was in Arizona in late August. The desert floor far below would be baking in the searing sun, the same as in Las Vegas.

Nick nodded in approval. His travel agent had chosen well. This was exactly what he needed, a total change from Las Vegas and his job at the Miracles Casino. He was tired to the bone. For several weeks he had carried the responsibility of running Miracles alone while his boss and good friend, Jared Loring, had been on his honeymoon with his new wife, Tabor.

On the first leg of his two-week vacation, Nick had driven from Las Vegas to Houston to see his family and to pay a visit to Alison and Tucker Boone and their new son. Tucker was a silent partner with Jared in Miracles, leaving the running of the casino in Jared's capable hands. Nick was second in command under Jared, and they ran the place like a fine-tuned machine. The drive from Houston to Serenity Cove had been a killer, but he was here now, safe and sound. He was a mile high and light years from the world he lived in, and it was great. Pippa was great. No, forget Pippa. She was not part of the package his travel agent had arranged for him. Pippa Pauling was *not* vacation-fling material, and he would remember that. She was taboo, a keep-his-hands-in-his-pockets-and-off-Pippa Pauling.

"Oh, you're awake."

He turned and groaned silently when he saw Pippa standing across the room. She looked, darn it, even better now than when he'd been peering at her from flat on the floor. Oh, yes, she was lovely. He'd better Super Glue his hands into his pockets.

"I'm sort of awake." He ran his hand over his chin. "I need a shave, shower, and coffee. Then maybe I'll be human."

If he got any more human, Pippa thought dryly, she was going to faint. Nick looked even bigger, even more magnificent standing up and wearing jeans than he had flat on the floor in his undies. Her heart was doing the two-step again, drat it, and there was that odd, disturbing flutter of warmth within her. This would never do. She was getting her adolescent reactions to Nick Capoletti under control right now. She hoped.

"Just give me a few minutes to spruce up the bathroom and put out fresh towels," she said. "Why don't you unload your car while you're waiting?"

"Oh, no!" Nick smacked his forehead with the flat of his hand. "Where are my shoes? I left Peaches in the car all night."

Peaches? Pippa thought as Nick sat on the sofa and slipped on his shoes. Who was Peaches? A woman? No, that was silly. A dog or a cat? Who was Peaches?

"Who is Peaches?" she asked. Not that it was any of her business, but . . .

"My African violet," Nick said, striding toward the door.

She blinked. "Peaches is a plant?"

He stopped at the door and turned toward her. "Not just a plant, an African violet in full bloom. She's a beauty, but very delicate. I shouldn't have left her in the car all night. She's actually Peaches the Second. The first Peaches was drowned when the sprinkler system was set off so Jared could get a jump on Mickey the Mouse, who was holding Tabor captive. That all turned out just fine, and Tabor and Jared are married now. Peaches the First gave her life for the cause. Really bummed me out, but Tabor got me Peaches the Second, so I'd better go get her." He hurried out the door.

Pippa stood very still for a moment, then shook her head with the hope that it might help her understand

Nick's explanation. No, it didn't help a bit. If there had been any rhyme or reason to what Nick had said, she'd missed it completely. Except, of course, that Peaches was an African violet, and she was a beauty. As for the rest of his spiel? Forget it; it hadn't made one bit of sense. Well, rather than chalk him up as being totally insane, which would be a rotten shame and terribly frightening, she'd just have to assume that Nick had understood everything he'd said.

"Pippa!" he yelled from the front porch. "Would you open the door, please? I need both hands to hold Peaches."

Of course, he did, Pippa thought. Peaches was a seven-foot tall African violet and weighed two hundred pounds. The way things had been going so far that morning, nothing would have surprised her.

When she opened the door, Nick smiled at her and carefully stepped into the cabin. Nestled in his large hands was a lovely African violet in a milk-glass pot. Moving as though he were carrying a dozen fragile eggs, he walked toward the kitchen. Pippa watched him, a smile tugging at her lips.

Nick Capoletti, she mused, was an unusual man. He obviously cared a great deal about his violet named Peaches, and wasn't worried about who knew it. She'd never known a man who was so self-assured that he'd risk being considered unmasculine by showering attention and affection on a delicate flowering plant. How very different Nick was from—No, she wasn't racing back in time to compare Nick to Bill. Bill was of a different era and long past. Nick was in the here and now. Temporarily, of course.

Ordering herself to go clean the bathroom, Pippa closed the door and started across the room. Of their own volition, though, her bare feet took her to the kitchen, where she saw Nick, with his hands on hips, looking at Peaches, the window, then back at the plant.

"All set?" she asked.

"Yep. If she sits there in the middle of the table, she ought to get just enough sun."

Pippa walked over to him. "It really is a lovely plant, Nick."

He continued to stare at Peaches, a serious expression on his face. "I suppose it's kind of nuts for a guy to be all charged up over a violet. I bought the first Peaches over a year ago, when I moved to Las Vegas. I did it on impulse, thinking it would give a homey touch to my living room. Then . . . I don't know . . . it struck me as time passed that if I didn't water it, tend it, care about it, it would die. I'd never been responsible for anyone, or anything, like that before. I liked the feeling that I was important, that my being there made a difference." He paused and cleared his throat. "Forget it. You'll think I'm totally weird."

She placed one hand on his forearm. "Oh, no, not at all. What you just said was very nice. There are men who don't want to be responsible for anything, not even themselves. Peaches is a fortunate plant, and I've never seen anything as pretty sitting on that table."

Nick looked down at Pippa's hand resting on his arm. Her fingers were small and delicate, her touch gentle. Her skin was pale next to his own, which was naturally swarthy, due to his Italian heritage, and darkened more by the desert sun. The warmth from Pippa's hand was spreading through him, and he slowly shifted his eyes to meet Pippa's gaze.

He was in trouble, he thought. The urge to kiss Pippa's luscious lips was nearly overpowering. All he had to do was lean down and claim her mouth to be able to taste her, inhale her delicate aroma even more. He would draw her to him and feel all of her, not just her hand, pressed against him. He was so incredibly aware of every delectable inch of her, and strangely conscious of every inch of himself as well. He had to move back from her. Right away.

Nick didn't move.

He wanted to kiss her, Pippa thought. She could see it in his eyes, in the way his gaze flickered over her lips. And she wanted him to kiss her, wanted to feel his mouth on hers, wanted to be held tightly in those strong arms. Heat swirled within her; pulsing, demanding heat. Her senses had sharpened, magnifying the feel of the soft hair on his arm and the steely muscles beneath his skin. This was bizarre, frightening, not remotely like anything she'd experienced before. She had to move away from this man.

Pippa didn't move.

"I'm going to kiss you," Nick said, his voice raspy.

"I know," she whispered.

He leaned down slowly, weaving his fingers through her silky dark hair. His gaze traced her features, coming to rest on her lips. He moved his hands forward to frame her face, one thumb sliding over the sprinkling of freckles on her nose. He looked into her eyes again, and had to remind himself to breathe.

Magic, he thought. This woman had cast a magic spell over him. The anticipation of the kiss was sweet torture, a lingering between heaven and hell. And it was only a kiss, he told himself, yet he felt as though he were standing on the brink of a momentous discovery, a major change in his life.

He lowered his head and brushed his lips over Pippa's.

A rush of disappointment swept through Pippa as Nick's mouth touched hers for just an instant, giving her only the faintest taste and feel of him. Her legs were trembling, threatening to refuse to support her.

How could a simple kiss wreak such havoc with her sense of reasoning, spark this heated desire within her? she wondered. Nick's brief caress wasn't enough, not nearly enough. He had to kiss her, really kiss her, now!

As if in answer to her silent demand, he kissed one corner of her mouth, then the other. She shivered. He slid his tongue along her bottom lip, and her eyes drifted closed. At last his mouth melted over hers, his tongue parting her lips and delving inside. This, he knew instantly, had been worth waiting for. This was worth the ache in his body as his manhood stirred. This kiss was ambrosia.

Her arms floated up to circle his neck, and his dropped to wrap around her waist, gathering her close. Eagerly, hungrily, she met his tongue and the increasing demands of his mouth, drinking in the taste and feel of him. Her fingers inched into his thick black hair, urging his lips harder onto hers. She was awash with desire, with an intense need she couldn't restrain. She could feel Nick's arousal heavy against her, and gloried in knowing he wanted her as much as she wanted him. She was floating in a sea of wondrous sensations, some long forgotten, some never known.

He was slipping to the edge of his control, Nick thought. That a kiss could create such driving passion within him was unbelievable . . . and fantastic. He'd waited a lifetime for magic such as this, and had begun to fear he'd never find it. But here it was, and here she was, and the magic was there.

But this was Pippa, he told himself hazily. Different and special, not like the women he knew. She was real. And she was vulnerable, with an intriguing aura of innocence about her. He mustn't frighten her, mustn't rush her. He mustn't shatter the magic.

He lifted his head, his breathing rough. "Pippa. Pippa, we . . . I have to stop. I really . . . have to stop kissing you."

She slowly opened her eyes. "Oh." She stared up at him, and an expression of horror crept onto her face. "Oh!" She took a step backward, then another, swaying slightly. Her hands flew to her flushed cheeks. "Oh, dear heaven, what have I done? What did you do? What did we . . . ? I can't believe this. I have never—I don't do things like this."

"Look," Nick said, reaching out his hand to her, "I—"

"No." Shaking her head, she stepped back farther.

He dropped his hand to his side. "Pippa, don't. Don't spoil what we shared by getting upset."

"Upset?" she repeated, her voice rising. "I'm mortified, totally ashamed of myself. You must think I'm a—"

"Very lovely, very special woman," he interrupted quietly. "That kiss, Pippa Pauling, was magic. That's the word that best describes it. Magic. There's something happening between us, Pippa."

"There is not!" Her glance fell below his waist for a moment, and the flush on her cheeks deepened. "It's very obvious what happened *between* us."

"I don't mean *that*," he said loudly. He raised his hands in a gesture of peace, and his tone was gentle when he spoke again. "Just calm down, okay? We didn't do anything wrong. In fact, it was so right, it blows my mind. That kiss was sensational. Can't we just leave it at that?" He paused. "For now."

She narrowed her eyes. "What does that mean, that tacked-on 'for now'?"

"Nothing," he said quickly. He flashed her a bright smile. "Okay? Are you calm? There's really nothing to be upset about."

She pressed one hand to her forehead. "I'm going to erase this whole thing from my brain. I'm going to go clean the bathroom and forget this ever happened."

"Well, thanks a helluva lot," he said, his smile changing to a frown. "It's really great to hear that my kiss is going to be replaced with memories of scrubbing the john." He folded his arms over his chest. "That's really insulting."

"Well, I'm sorry, but I *have* to forget it. If I don't, I might . . ." Her voice trailed off.

"Yes?" he asked, raising his eyebrows. "You might what? Decide you'd like another one of those kisses? Or two? Or a dozen? Hmm?"

"You're starting to sound conceited."

"I am *not* conceited. I'm charming. I'm a very charming Italian man, who respects and admires women, holds them in high esteem. Ask anyone who knows me, and they'll tell you how charming I am. Call my mother; she'll vouch for me." He paused, and his expression became serious. "Don't be frightened by what happened here, Pippa. I'm not going to hurt you. There's nothing to be afraid of. Don't you see that?"

"No," she whispered. "It shouldn't have happened, and it won't happen again." She spun around and hurried out of the room.

"Dandy," Nick muttered, dragging a hand through his hair. "She's on her way to flush the memory of that kiss down the old commode."

It had been a special kiss, he mused, staring off into

who faced life head on, the good and the bad. She changed what she could and resigned herself to what she couldn't. She didn't fantasize about the might-have-beens or distress herself with a list of "if-onlys." She was pleased and proud of what she'd accomplished for herself and Emma. She was happy and totally contented.

Wasn't she?

Yes, of course she was.

Then why, she asked herself yet again, had she been behaving so strangely since her first glimpse of Nick Capoletti in his blue undies? What was it about him—other than his fabulous body, raw virility, knock-'em-dead smile, and gorgeous face—that had pushed some unknown button within her?

Oh, she didn't know. All she was certain of was that it would not happen again. She was once more on schedule, her mind and body back under her command. What a relief.

Finished with that bedroom, she headed toward the door with the intention of readying the second one. She gasped and stopped dead in her tracks as Nick's massive frame filled the doorway. He smiled at her, holding a suitcase in one hand and wearing only a towel tucked low on his narrow hips.

TWO

Emotions tumbled through Pippa with such speed that she didn't have time to react to one before the next slammed into her. Shock whizzed by, a flash of desire, a tingle of excitement, a dab of fear, then anger. Her emotional gauge got stuck right there, on anger.

With, she reluctantly admitted, a bit of desire that hadn't totally dissipated. The sight of Nick's broad, tanned chest, the dark curly hair glistening with moisture, was making her light-headed. Beneath his trim waist, an arrow of dark hair pointed to treasures hidden by the towel. His bare legs she'd seen before, but a rerun glimpse did nothing to diminish the impact of their powerful build. His face was clean-shaven, his hair damp and shiny. He was so gorgeous, it was a sin.

But she didn't care! No, sir, she told herself. As soon as she figured out where the anger had disappeared to, she was going to give Mr. Capoletti a piece of her mind.

"Don't let me interrupt your work," he said. "I'll just get dressed. You won't even know I'm here."

Aha, Pippa thought. She'd found the anger.

She planted her fists on her hips. "How dare you traipse around like that? What kind of place do you think I'm running here?"

He frowned. "I'm not traipsing. I'm entering my bedroom to get dressed, like a normal, socially modest person."

"There's another bedroom, you know."

"With no sheets on the bed, which means you haven't been in there yet, which means I'd be in your way and disrupt your schedule. Here I am, trying to be a considerate guest, attempting not to upset your routine, and you accuse me of traipsing. Really, Pippa, you're not being very nice."

"Oh," she said in a small voice. "I . . . well . . . I'm sorry."

"That's okay. I'm charming, remember? I don't hold grudges." He walked into the room and flipped the suitcase up onto the bed. "I have a lot of luggage because I was visiting in Houston before I came here. I think my casual clothes are in this one." He snapped the suitcase open. "Yep, here we go."

"The afternoon will be warm, but the nights are chilly," she said absently. She'd apologized to him? Yes, that was what she'd done, all right. How had it gotten all turned around like that? He *had* traipsed in half-naked, knowing she was there, darn it. "I'll get out of your way." She started toward the door.

"You're not in my way." She stopped and glanced back at him. "This is a great room. In fact, I like the whole cabin. It has a homey touch. This bedroom suits you. You look good in here. We look good in here, together. Don't you think we fit in this bedroom together just fine, Pippa?"

He started walking toward her, and she couldn't look away, couldn't move. He stopped directly in front of her, and she filled her senses with his fresh, soapy aroma. The heat was back, deep within her.

He lifted one hand and fiddled with a lock of her hair near her cheek. "I don't want you to be afraid of me, Pippa," he said in a low voice. "Not ever. If I do something that disturbs or frightens you, tell me and I'll stop." His thumb feathered across her lips. "See? I'm harmless. There's nothing threatening about me. I don't have"—he lowered his head toward hers—"a threatening bone in my body."

Was he crazy? she wondered deliriously. He was threatening to the entire female population simply by breathing. He was . . . He was . . . He was kissing her.

His mouth claimed hers and all rational thought fled. Only his lips and one hand were touching her, yet her entire body was on fire with need. His tongue slipped into her mouth, and she welcomed it, stroked it with her own. Her breasts seemed to swell with desire, and the heat within her pulsed with an insistent rhythm.

Nick lifted his head, dropped his hand, and stepped back. "There," he said hoarsely. "You don't have any reason to be afraid of me."

"The bed," she murmured.

"What?"

She blinked, then stiffened. "I have to go make up the other bed. Right now." She turned and nearly ran out of the room, pulling the door closed behind her.

Nick released a long breath and sank onto the edge of the bed. That kiss had just about tapped out his present supply of willpower and restraint. Whew! He'd wanted to pull Pippa close, cup her breasts in his hands, stroke her long, satiny legs. . . . But he'd been brave, courageous, and bold, mustering his control, and stepping away from her before things had gotten out of hand. Lord knew he didn't want to scare her to death. She was skittish, and, understandably, didn't trust him as far as she could throw him. He was really going to have to take this slow and easy.

He dressed in khaki shorts and a brown knit shirt, then rummaged through the suitcase for clean socks. Suitably dressed, he left the bedroom in search of Pippa. He found her in the kitchen, and she glanced up as he entered.

"I made you some coffee," she said. "The people who had the cabin before you left some behind. Did your travel agent tell you that we have a small store here, where you can buy supplies?"

"He mentioned it, I think," Nick said, pouring himself a mug of coffee. "I was very busy at the time, and just told him to take care of things."

"When he made your reservation, he gave his agency in Las Vegas as your address. You'll need to fill out a registration card with your own address, who to notify in case of an emergency, that sort of thing. If you prefer to drive into town, you can buy your supplies there."

"Down that mountain? Forget it." He sat at the table. "Hello, Peaches. How's life in the pines? I'll shop at your store."

"Whatever suits you. There are rowboats by the lake and fishing tackle is available. The four other cabins are occupied, so you'll probably run into other people. Emma and I live in cabin one. This is cabin two. Grandma and Grandpa Pauling live in the back of the store."

He looked up at her. "Grandma and Grandpa Pauling? They're your in-laws?"

"They're my ex-husband's parents, yes."

"Where is your . . . their son?"

"I have no idea." She pushed herself away from the counter, fixing her gaze somewhere above his head. "You're all set here, clean as a whistle. I'll drop by later with your registration card. I hope you enjoy your stay at Serenity Cove, Mr. Capoletti. Please feel free to call on me, or Grandma and Grandpa Pauling, for any assistance you may need. We're here to make your vacation as pleasurable as possible."

"How long?" Nick asked quietly.

She met his gaze. "You don't know how long your vacation is? Your travel agent reserved the cabin for one week."

"Yes, I realize that. I meant, how long has it been since you've heard from your ex-husband?"

"I really don't think that's any of your business," she said, a slight edge to her voice. "I must be going. I'm behind schedule."

She started across the room, but he grasped her hand as she passed him. "How long?"

She looked at his large hand trapping hers, then glared at him. "You're rude."

"I'm charming," he said smiling. "Answer the question."

"Why?"

"Because I want to know. I want to know everything I can about you, Pippa, and this is as good a place as any to start." He paused. "How's this? You answer my question, and I'll answer one of yours about me. Even trade. Tit for tat."

"I can ask anything I want?"

"Well, now, wait a minute. Let's keep this fair. It has

to be within the same general topic range. At the moment we're discussing ex-husbands."

"You have one?" she asked blandly, pulling her hand free.

"No! You can ask me one question about my ex-whatevers."

"Lovely title you give them," she said, shaking her head. Nick shrugged. "Okay, why not? William, known as Bill, Pauling, flew the coop when I was three months pregnant with Emma. I was nineteen at the time. I waited several months for him to come back. He didn't, I filed for divorce, and that was that. End of story."

"That stinks. The guy is scum."

"He was a child afraid to take on the responsibility of the child he'd helped to create."

"So he ran out on you, and you never heard from him again?"

"One question, remember? All right, let's see. Have you ever been married?"

"No."

"Why not?"

"Sorry, chum." He grinned. "One question per customer. Want to go another round?"

"No, I'm late. I've got to go."

"Ah, yes, your schedule."

"My schedule is what keeps this place running smoothly," she said stiffly. "Grandma and Grandpa are getting on in years. They count on me to see that Serenity Cove maintains the high reputation they worked so hard to earn over the past twenty years."

"How long have you been here at Serenity Cove?"

"You've used up your one question . . . chum. Ta-ta."

She turned and left the kitchen. Nick watched her go, admiring her enticing bottom and wonderful legs.

After he heard the door shut behind her, he sipped his hot coffee and considered what he knew about her.

She had been married to a jerk who'd run out on her when she was very young and pregnant. William Pauling was a creep. Check. The senior Paulings must have recognized their son for the sleaze that he was and encouraged Pippa and Emma at some time to make their home there at Serenity Cove. Check.

He also knew Pippa was a passionate woman, yet she did not seem comfortable with, or maybe wasn't even aware of, her own sensuality. He had frightened her, and he sensed she was ready to cut and run if he threatened her scheduled, organized existence in any way. Check.

"And she kisses like a dream, Peaches," he said to the violet. "Her body fits mine as if she were custom-ordered for me. There's magic between Pippa and me. The tricky part is to figure out if it's the forever kind of magic."

He drained his mug, then carried his remaining suitcases from the living room to the bedroom. After unpacking what he thought he'd need for a stay on the top of a mountain, he walked out onto his front porch. He filled his lungs with air that was so crisp and clean, it almost seemed to have a foreign taste.

He wondered absently if his body was going to go into pollution withdrawal, as he gazed at the magnificent, towering pines. The scenery was so perfect, it could have been painted. And it was incredibly quiet. He could actually hear birds singing in the trees. It was soothing there, peaceful. Serenity Cove had been well named. After the madness of Las Vegas and the hubbub of Houston, this tranquility was welcome.

He glanced at the inviting padded lounge chair on

the porch and toyed with the idea of stretching out for a nap, then decided he'd better find the store Pippa had told him about and stock his cupboards.

His hands in his pockets, he wandered leisurely along the cleared path. It wandered through the pines, and more trails branched off in various directions. Some, he surmised, must go to the other cabins and the lake, and some might be walking paths for those who wanted to go for a stroll.

The winding trail soon brought him to a cottage like his, with a sign by the door that said, "Cabin One." Pippa and Emma's house, he mused, continuing on. Was Pippa in there? No, probably not. He doubted that her ever-famous schedule included taking a break, sitting in a comfortable chair in her living room with her feet up.

The next building he saw was bigger and boasted a sign stating, "General Store." He crossed the porch and pushed open the door. A bell tinkled, and he grinned.

Stepping into the store, he instantly decided he'd been transported back in time. With its floor-to-ceiling shelves jam-packed with anything and everything, the store was straight out of the early West. There was even a potbelly stove in the center of the room with a few chairs pulled up to it. Glass jars filled with an enticing assortment of candy stood in a row on the counter. Behind the counter was a short, thin, gray-haired woman, appearing to be in her late sixties, and who looked like the quintessential grandmother. Emma's grandmother, he imagined.

"Hello," the woman said, smiling at him.

"Hi." He walked over to the counter. "This is a great

store, right out of the history books." He extended his hand. "I'm Nick Capoletti."

The woman shook his hand. "Just call me Grandma. Everyone does. Tradition says that when you come in the store for the first time, you help yourself to a piece of candy. Take your pick."

"Red licorice." He took the lid off the jar and pulled out a long, thin piece of the treat.

Grandma laughed. "You're a man who knows his own mind. I've seen some who study those jars for a long time, trying to decide what to have."

"I know what I want when I see it," he said, and took a bite of licorice.

Grandma studied him. "Yes, I'd say that you do. Question is, do you also get what you want?"

He chuckled. "No, but you can believe I sure give it my best shot before I give anything up as a lost cause."

"Oh, I do like you, Nick Capoletti," Grandma said, beaming. "Welcome to Serenity Cove."

"Thank you, ma'am. I'm glad to be here. My life has been rather hectic lately, and this is exactly what I need."

"Where are you from?"

"Houston, originally. I've lived in Las Vegas for the past year or so."

"Las Vegas." Grandma clicked her tongue. "Such stories I've heard about the goings-on there. Aren't you afraid you'll be bored here?"

"Not for a minute. There are some very interesting attractions here." Thinking of Pippa, he couldn't keep a smile from curving his mouth. "Very interesting."

Once more Grandma studied him, then she nodded. "Tread softly, Nick Capoletti. Things rushed have a way of turning out poorly."

They were talking about Pippa, Nick thought. He knew it, and Grandma knew it. She hadn't pulled a gun from beneath the counter to warn him to stay away from her daughter-in-law. In fact, she was giving him advice, telling him to go slow and easy with Pippa, which he'd already figured out on his own. Well, chalk one up for the Italian kid from Vegas. It would seem that Grandma Pauling just might be in his corner.

"I'll tread softly, Grandma," he said, smiling warmly at her.

"I'll be watching."

"I'm sure you will. Well, I'd better get some food," he said, glancing around. "I'll just buy what I can carry in one trip. That way, I can come visit you and the red licorice more often."

Grandma laughed. "Good plan."

"Time will tell," he said, winking.

He wandered away from the counter, and was soon caught up in exploring the multitude of treasures on the shelves of the quaint store.

It was well over an hour later before he was back in his kitchen, putting away the last of his supplies. He made himself a thick sandwich of ham, cheese, lettuce, and tomato, all generously slathered with mayonnaise. With that and a tall glass of milk, he settled into the cushioned lounge on the front porch.

When he was through eating, he slouched lower in the chair, laced his fingers loosely on his chest, and within minutes was asleep.

Late that afternoon, Pippa slowly approached Nick's cabin. She knew she was postponing being face-to-face with Nick Capoletti again, and chided herself for her childish behavior.

If only she'd been able to erase from her brain the events of that morning, she thought. But instead the remembrance of the kisses shared with Nick, the feel of his mouth, his arms, his body, and the startling sensations that had whirled through her, all stayed in her mind. Like a vivid, larger-than-life movie, everything had replayed over and over, the details growing sharper every time.

How had it all happened? she asked herself yet again. What had become of her ability to think and reason, to know right from wrong? She'd never behaved so . . . so wantonly before. She'd grown adept at sidestepping the advances of the men who came to Serenity Cove for a weekend of fishing and hiking. She'd learned how to make it clear, politely but firmly, that she was not part of the entertainment package.

She stopped and looked at Cabin Two. She'd kissed Nick Capoletti, she thought dismally. And she'd enjoyed every exciting, frightening moment. Never before had she felt such instant, burning desire raging through her like an uncontrollable fire. All she had to do was allow her mind to linger for a moment on the crystal-clear memories, and the heat would swell within her once again. Such disgraceful behavior.

Well, she knew one thing was certain. It wasn't going to happen again. She was going to stay out of Nick's way, and most definitely out of his arms, for the next week. Then he'd leave, and her life would return to its set, normal routine, with its schedules keeping things running smoothly. Each day would follow its usual pattern.

Its usual boring pattern.

Pippa stiffened. What? Where had the word *boring* come from? That was insane. She wasn't bored with her life at Serenity Cove. She loved it there, had for years. It gave her the sense of stability and permanence she'd been seeking for so long. She had a real family, had Emma and Grandma and Grandpa Pauling. She was contented and at peace. Darn it, she wasn't bored!

She started off again, her tennis shoes thudding on the dirt path. Oh, she'd be glad when this day was over and she could start fresh in the morning. From the moment she'd seen Nick sleeping on the floor, she hadn't been behaving like herself. This newest, absurd thought that her life was boring was the last straw.

She stomped up the porch steps of cabin two, then halted when she saw Nick sound alseep in the lounge chair.

And there, she fumed, staring at him, was the source of her unsettling, crummy day. There, looking so incredibly gorgeous, it was enough to make a woman weep. It was all Nick, Mr. Charming Italian, Capoletti's fault.

Pippa sighed. No, it wasn't, she admitted. He was part of it, but he hadn't forced her to kiss him. He certainly hadn't held a gun to her head and demanded she respond to those kisses in total abandon. She'd done that part all on her own, brazen person that she'd been. Well, no more of that stuff.

" 'Lo," Nick said, not opening his eyes. "We have to quit meeting like this, Pippa, or people will talk. I fall asleep, you show up in my bedroom."

"This is a porch, Mr. Capoletti," she said stiffly. "And this morning it was a living room."

"Mere technicalities." He opened his eyes, groaned,

and glanced at his watch. "I slept the afternoon away. I guess I was even more bushed than I realized."

"Well, remember the air is thinner up here. Some people find they tire easily for the first day or so, even if they arrive well rested."

"I'm rejuvenated now," he said, sitting up. "Raring to go and eager to get on with it."

It? she wondered. What "it"? Was there a sexual innuendo in that statement? Oh, for Pete's sake, she was getting paranoid.

He smiled at her. "Is this a social call? How nice. Would you care for something to drink?"

"No, thank you, and no, this isn't a social call." She shoved a white card at him. "I'd appreciate it if you'd fill out this registration card and give it to Grandma at the store."

He took the card, but didn't look at it. "Shouldn't I give it to you?"

"Grandma will see that I get it. I'm very busy, and hard to find at times. Well, have a nice evening. Good-bye." She started to go.

"Hey, wait a minute." He swung his feet around and stood up. "What's your rush? Why don't you stay and chat awhile?"

Pippa continued down the steps, then turned to look at him. "Thank you, but no. I have to go check to see if all the boats are in. Then it will be time to start dinner. It's important that Emma can count on a stable routine. It gives a child a tremendous sense of security."

"Well, yeah, I suppose," Nick said, "but spontaneity, surprises, can be fun too. Schedules and routines don't have to be etched in stone, you know."

"Not while on vacation, the way you are, but we live here. This is our day-to-day life."

"I know, but—"

"I must go. Emma is waiting for me."

"Yeah, okay. I'll see you tomorrow."

"Oh, maybe not," Pippa said, waving a hand breezily. "I have a lot to do. We might not run into each other."

"Pippa, I *will* see you tomorrow."

She lifted her chin and met his gaze. "Am I supposed to ask if that's a promise or a threat?"

"No. It's a simple statement of fact."

It was? Pippa wondered, unable to look away from him. Then why did she feel slightly threatened, as well as excited? And why was that heat creeping through her again, demanding attention? Darn that Nick with his deep, sexy voice and his mesmerizing dark eyes. Now her feet were refusing to move at her command, her heart was thudding crazily, and . . . just darn him.

" 'Bye," she said, and hurried away, amazing herself with her ability to tear her gaze from his.

Nick leaned his shoulder against the post of the porch and watched her go. Pippa was as skittish as a colt, he mused. She also worked too hard. Grandma Pauling was pushing seventy, and he imagined Grandpa was too. Unless someone came in to help from town, Pippa was doing everything except running the store. The trails he'd walked had been free of weeds and debris, she'd cleaned his cabin, she'd spoken of having made up a shopping list, and now she was going to check on the boats.

He shook his head. What about general repair and upkeep of the cabins? he wondered. Who handled the reservations, the accounting books? And in addition to everything else, Pippa had a child to raise. It was too much, it really was. Of course, he didn't know for certain that she did it all alone, but it was sure beginning to look as though she did.

He stretched out on the lounge again, lacing his fingers behind his head. What about Pippa, the woman? he wondered. Did she have any time just for herself, to do what *she* wanted to do? With so many responsibilities resting on her shoulders, did she even truly know what those wants and needs might be? How long had it been since she'd had some plain old fun, laughed right out loud, grabbed some hours and claimed them as hers to enjoy as she pleased? She'd probably say that kind of thing wasn't on her schedule.

"Well," Nick said to no one, "we'll see about that."

It was after eleven when Pippa put down the pen, closed the ledger, and leaned back in the chair, massaging her aching temples.

Serenity Cove was getting in deeper and deeper financial trouble, she thought dismally. She'd cut corners everywhere she could think of without compromising the reputation the Paulings had worked so hard to achieve. She now did all the repairs within her capabilities, kept the grounds clean and attractive, readied the cabins for arriving guests, kept track of what needed restocking in the store.

Still, they were slowly but surely losing financial ground. She had to continue the high cost of advertising, mailing the expensive color brochures to travel agencies across the country. Word of mouth would no longer keep the cabins booked solid. The summers were still busy, but each winter they had fewer and fewer guests. They couldn't compete with the ski resorts and fancy hotels once the snow came. If this winter brought in as little money as the last one, Serenity Cove would be finished.

Tears blurred Pippa's vision, and she shook her head. What was she going to do? How could she tell the Paulings that their years of work could very well be for nothing? She owed them so much, was so grateful to them for having made a home for her and Emma years before. Grandma and Grandpa had no idea Serenity Cove was in trouble, and her heart ached with the thought of having to break the horrifying news to them.

Maybe, she thought, this winter would be better than the last one. More people would come, the cabins would be full, and—No, she was kidding herself. She'd done everything possible to keep Serenity Cove afloat, but it hadn't been enough. The Paulings could sell the land and have a fairly comfortable retirement somewhere.

But what about her and Emma? Where would they go? How would she support Emma, provide a decent home for her precious daughter? Serenity Cove had been the perfect solution for a young mother with only a high-school diploma. She had a family there, a sense of belonging and stability. She worked hard, but it was worth every minute, since she was always close to her child and didn't have to leave her with strangers during the day. Emma was a happy, bubbly little girl, who was secure in the knowledge that her mother would be there whenever she needed her.

And now? Pippa wondered as she stood. Emma would be starting first grade down in town in a few weeks, and was so excited about her upcoming birthday and the prospect of going to first grade with the other "big kids." How could she tell her, or the Paulings, that probably before the winter was out, Serenity Cove would have to be sold to one of the developers who was always sniffing around, and they would all have to move off their mountain?

"I need a magic wand," Pippa muttered. Magic. That was the word Nick had used to describe their kisses. Magic. There was no such thing. Yes, all right, what she'd felt while being kissed by Nick was like nothing she'd ever experienced before. It had been special, different, wonderful. But magic? A lovely word, a make-believe word that represented what really wasn't. Reality was stark and honest. There would be no more kisses shared with Nick Capoletti, and in the near future there would be no more Serenity Cove.

"Oh, God," Pippa whispered, "what am I going to do?"

Tears fell onto her cheeks, and she angrily dashed them away. She had no time for weeping, she told herself, or for self-pity. Tomorrow she had to check the roofs on all the cabins, and she was dreading what she would find. Two fishing poles had been returned that day with tangled lines that would take time and patience to unravel. The flower beds in front of each cabin needed weeding. The drains—

"Go to bed, Pippa," she said, interrupting her own thoughts. "Things aren't going to get any better by dwelling on them." Except the remembrance of Nick's kisses. Those memories just kept getting better and better and—"Good night, Pippa Pauling!"

She locked up the cabin, turned off the lights, and made her way slowly down the hall in the darkness. In her room she snapped on the lamp by her bed, then walked across the hall to check on Emma.

So sweet, she thought, gazing down at her daughter. Though he had done little else, Bill had helped her create a miracle. How she loved Emma. She wanted so much for her. Not just in a material sense, but more—the really important things. She wanted Emma to have order in her life, security, a feeling of continuity and permanence. She wanted Emma to wake up each morning knowing there would be a sensible structure to her day, one without unpleasant, disconcerting surprises.

Pippa straightened Emma's blanket, then kissed her gently on the forehead. Serenity Cove had been so perfect for Emma, she thought, and it was the only home her daughter remembered having. She didn't want to take Emma away, leave the mountain and all it offered to her child. But if things continued as they were, she'd have no choice. They'd have to go.

If only, Pippa mused, there were really such a thing as magic.

Three

The next day was cool and cloudy, and Nick dressed in jeans and a sweatshirt. Despite his long nap the previous afternoon, he had slept well, deciding the bed was infinitely more comfortable than the living-room floor.

While he ate a breakfast of scrambled eggs, toast, and coffee, he carried on a lengthy conversation with Peaches, being a firm believer in the theory that a plant talked to was a happy, healthy plant.

As he set his dishes in the sink, he heard a strange thud that rattled the window over the sink. He opened the back door of the cabin to investigate, and what he saw brought an instant frown to his face.

A ladder was propped against the cabin. He strode to the bottom of it and looked up. Pippa was at the top, leaning onto the roof, bent at the waist. While Nick admitted the view from his vantage point was extremely enticing, and Pippa Pauling in snug jeans was a lovely sight to behold, he was still none too happy about her precarious perch on the rickety ladder.

"Hey!" he yelled. "What are you doing up there?"

"Aaak!" she screamed, straightening so fast that the ladder began to wobble.

"Lord." He quickly grabbed the ladder to steady it.

Pippa planted her gloved hands flat on the roof and glowered down at Nick. "You scared the bejeebers out of me, Nick Capoletti. I was trying to be quiet in case you were still asleep, but you yell loudly enough to wake the dead."

"Fine," he said gruffly. "Now answer the question. What are you doing up there?"

"Checking the roof."

"Trust me, it's still there. Get down here before you break your neck."

"No." She turned and crawled up onto the roof.

"Dammit," he muttered.

He tested his weight on the first rung of the ladder, then climbed up the rungs slowly, not convinced the old wood was capable of supporting his two hundred pounds. When he reached the top, he saw Pippa scrambling across the roof on her hands and knees.

"Hey!" he said, as loudly as before.

"Aaak!" she screamed again. She glanced back at him. "Would you cut that out? This is scary enough without your hollering every two seconds."

He looked down at the ground, then at Pippa again. "Damn right, it's scary. Why are we up here?"

"*We* are not up here, *I* am, and I already told you, I'm checking the roof." Her gaze swept over the surface. "Dear heavens."

"What's wrong?"

"Stay on that ladder. If you come on the roof, you'll probably go right through. It's worse than I thought."

She inched her way back toward him, and Nick's gaze was riveted to her wiggling bottom.

"How am I doing?" she asked.

"Fantastic," he said. "What?"

"Am I close to the ladder?"

"I'll guide you. Just keep backing up." Leaning forward, he looked heavenward in thanks, then curved one hand around Pippa's hip.

"What do you think you're doing? Get your big paw off me."

"Fear not, ma'am," he said, chuckling. "Everything is under control." Except his libido. "A little to the right. That's it. Keep coming. What a team we make." He grasped her left calf.

"Nick, it's not necessary to—"

"We're doing fine. A little more." He guided her foot onto the top rung of the ladder, then reluctantly removed his hand from her hip and slid her other foot to the rung. "There."

Pippa's backside was now wiggling toward the center of his chest, and he gazed at it rather wistfully.

"I'll go on down," he said. "I don't think this ladder will support both of us. Be careful, for crying out loud."

" 'Kay."

He reached the ground, then watched as Pippa descended. When she was within reach, he gripped her at the waist and lifted her onto the ground.

"Thank you," she said, pulling off her gloves. "That wasn't fun. Actually, it was terrifying, but at least I'm finished. Yours was the last to be checked."

"Geez, Pippa, you could have fallen. Why were you checking all the roofs?"

She sighed, looking up at him. Well, hello, Nick, she

thought. Hello, magnificent Nick. He really was such a beautiful man.

"Pippa?"

"What?" She blinked. "Oh, the roofs. They're not in good shape, not one of them. Between age, the winter snows, and the summer rains, they're shot. I'm surprised they haven't started leaking before now. I didn't think they were in this bad shape."

"You'll have to have them all repaired?"

"No." She looked down at her gloves rather than up at him.

"Totally replaced?"

She shook her head. "No."

He extended one long finger, placed it under her chin, and lifted her head. A strange pain gripped his chest as he saw tears shimmering in her green eyes.

"Pippa?" he asked gently, framing her face with both hands. "Talk to me. Lousy roofs make you cry? What's going on here?"

"Nothing is going on," she said, trying to blink away her tears.

"Yeah, right. Climbing on roofs is an emotionally moving experience. Would you tell me what's wrong?"

"It's not your problem."

"Your crying is my problem. Listen to me. I'm not here just to kiss you, you know. Not that I'd mind, of course, but there's more to it than that. If you've got a problem, then so do I. I want to know everything about you, and that doesn't mean only the good news. You're not alone. Do you hear me, Pippa Pauling? You're not alone."

She sniffled. "Oh, don't say that." Two big tears slid down her cheeks.

Nick swept them away with his thumbs. "Why not?

It's true. I'm right here, and I sincerely want to know why you're crying about roofs."

She managed a weak smile. "You make me sound like I'm nuts."

"You're sad, that's what you are. Come inside and have a cup of coffee. And don't say one word about having to stay on schedule." He dropped his hands and circled her shoulders with his arm, pulling her close to his side. "Come on."

Nick's arm felt so comforting, Pippa thought. So big and strong, so . . . there. *You're not alone.* Such wonderful words. What would it be like to be half of a whole, to have someone like Nick to share the bad times as well as the good? Someone to lean on as she was doing now. She was dreadfully tired, both physically and emotionally. *You're not alone.* Precious words, like a treasure to be cherished, never taken for granted. But words that in her case simply weren't true.

Inside the cabin, Nick settled Pippa in a chair at the table, and a moment later set a mug of coffee in front of her. He sat down opposite her and looked at her intently, his arms crossed on the table as he leaned toward her.

"Hello, Peaches," Pippa said, directing her attention to the violet. "So many pretty flowers."

"Look at me, Pippa."

"The leaves are like velvet, green velvet."

"Look . . . at . . . me."

She slowly shifted her gaze to meet his.

"Thank you," he said quietly. "Now, talk to me."

She shook her head.

He reached over to move her mug and gloves out of

the way, then took her hands in his. "Yes, Pippa, talk to me, share with me."

"No, Nick. Don't you see? This has nothing to do with you. You came here on vacation to relax and enjoy yourself, because that's what vacations are for. They're not for getting caught up in someone else's problems. You can't solve what's wrong. No one can."

"Maybe not, but you don't have to face it by yourself, whatever it is."

"Yes, I do," she whispered. "It's up to me. Your saying . . . your saying that I'm not alone sounded wonderful, but I *am* alone, and I mustn't forget that."

"Dammit, Pippa, I'm right here," he said firmly, tightening his grip on her hands. "You can see me, feel my hands holding yours. Please, Pippa, don't shut me out like this."

He couldn't bear the sight of her tears, the sorrow etched on her face, the smudges beneath her eyes that revealed her fatigue. She looked so fragile and vulnerable, and he wanted to scoop her into his arms and tell her that everything was going to be fine. He'd care for her and protect her. He'd . . . love her? Was he falling in love with Pippa Pauling? At very first sight? Well, second or third glimpse. "Pippa?"

"If I lean on you this time, what if—if I can't find the strength to stand on my own two feet again after you're gone?" she asked, her voice quivering.

He smiled. "We'll worry about that later. Let's start with the crummy roofs, okay? That's a good place. The cabins need new roofs, but . . ." He raised his brows questioningly.

She took a deep breath and let it out slowly. "But there's no money to fix them. There's no money for anything. I've been over the books a hundred times. We don't make enough in the summer to carry us through the winter, because we can't compete with the ski resorts. I haven't told Grandma and Grandpa Pauling how bad things are. They've worked for over twenty years to make Serenity Cove what it is. This will break their hearts. They'll have to sell out. There's no choice now, no hope. The roofs won't hold the weight of the snow for another winter. I owe the Paulings so much for what they've done for Emma and me. I've tried to make it all come together, but . . . Oh, I can't believe I'm dumping all this on you."

"You're not dumping, you're sharing. And I'm listening, Pippa, I really am."

"Thank you," she said softly. "I know there are no solutions to all of this, but I can't begin to tell you how much it meant to me to be able to pour it all out like that. It's been bottled up inside of me for so long, and I've been so worried. I'm going to have to tell the Paulings very soon. And Emma. I hate to do this to Emma. This is the only home she's ever known."

"How long have you been here?"

"Since Emma was six months old. Bill and I were married in San Diego, where I grew up. We didn't tell anyone. Bill said he was alone, had no family. I got pregnant a month after we were married, and he was furious. He blamed me for being careless and . . . Well, he just packed up and left when I was three months along."

Nick muttered an earthy expletive.

"Later, after I'd divorced Bill, I was sorting through some of the things he'd left behind. I found a picture of Grandma and Grandpa, and a letter from Grandma to Bill asking him to please keep in touch with them, let them know he was all right. She said she understood his not wanting to live at Serenity Cove, but they wanted at least to know where he was."

"So you answered the letter?"

"Not right away. I hadn't even known they existed, and I hated to write to strangers saying their son had run out on his pregnant bride. But when Emma was born I realized she was their granddaughter and they had the right to know about her. I sent them a picture of Emma, and just said that Bill and I were no longer married, without going into the details. I was struggling to support myself and Emma, but as the letters went back and forth between the Paulings and me I made it sound as though we were doing fine."

Nick stroked Pippa's knuckles with his thumbs as she spoke. A knot in his stomach kept twisting more tightly as her story unfolded. He could picture her: so young and frightened, trying desperately to care for her baby. While he'd never considered himself a violent person, he definitely would have liked to have ten minutes alone with Bill Pauling.

"Grandma and Grandpa were so eager to meet Emma and me, but I kept finding excuses for them not to come. I—I didn't want them to see the shabby place where we were living. They began to realize something was wrong, because I made the mistake of never mentioning Bill in any of the letters, didn't say he'd come to see Emma. They knew Bill was immature, and blamed themselves for spoiling him because they'd had him late in life, when they'd given up hope of ever having a child. They suspected he'd totally deserted me, and that I didn't want to tell them. They had someone from town take charge of Serenity Cove and came to San Diego without telling me they were coming."

"Good for them," Nick said.

"I was so tired, so scared, Nick. I was working as a waitress and leaving Emma with a neighbor. Emma had gotten an ear infection a week earlier, and my rent money had paid for the doctor and her medication. I was about to be evicted, when the Paulings arrived. They were wonderful. Before I knew it, Emma and I were on our way to our new home with our new family. We've been here ever since, and I'm so grateful to them for everything."

"You've more than earned your keep, Pippa. You work very hard here."

"It's little compared to what I've gotten in return, what Emma has gotten. We have a structure to our lives, a security we can count on."

He smiled. "And schedules."

"Yes, those too," she said, matching his smile. "They're important to me."

"Pippa, what about *your* family, *your* parents? Where were they when you were left all alone? Where are they now?"

"That's a whole other story." She pulled her hands free and pressed them to her cheeks. "I can't believe I sat here and poured my heart out to you like this. It isn't like me at all. I learned when I was very young to keep my feelings, my troubles, to myself, because I'm the only one who can fix them. Or if I can't fix them, then I accept things the way they are."

"Everyone needs a friend, Pippa."

"Friend? But you . . . that is . . ." Her voice trailed off.

He leaned back in his chair, his arms crossed over his chest. "I'm what? A man? Even more, I'm a man who has kissed you? Does that mean I don't qualify to be your friend because we've responded to each other on a man-to-woman level? Haven't you ever heard that your lover should also be your best friend?"

She shot to her feet. "You are not my lover."

Not yet, sweet Pippa, he thought. "I was making a point. You shouldn't stick me in a slot with a sign on my forehead that says I'm the guy who kisses the socks off you every chance I get, so I can't play any other role in your life. Pippa Pauling, I am your friend. A friend is someone you share with, good news and bad. Get it?"

She shook her head. "I don't know. I've never . . . Well, I've never had a real friend, I guess."

Nick slowly stood up, his eyes locked with Pippa's. "Well, you've got one now." He moved around the table, closing the distance between them. "I'm also," he went on, his voice seeming to drop an octave, "the man who kisses you every chance he gets." He gripped her lightly by the shoulders and turned her to face him.

"No. No, I—"

"Yes. Most definitely, yes."

His mouth melted over hers, and Pippa's lashes drifted down as her arms floated up to entwine his neck. Yes, yes, yes, she thought.

Nick gathered her close to his body, wrapping his arms tightly around her. Strong emotions tumbled through him, and heat thudded low and heavy within him. He felt torn between the need to make love to her for hours, and the need to protect her from harm, from sadness, from anything beyond the safe circle of his embrace.

He was Pippa's friend. And he would be her lover, he vowed. She was no longer alone, for he was there. Piece by piece, he was going to fit together the puzzle that was Pippa and discover who she was. Despite the rough times in her past, she seemed so damn innocent of the workings of the world, and of how it could be between a man and a woman. He was going to show her, teach her. He would lead her to a place where she could laugh, and sing, and shout with joy. Because she was special, so very special.

He raised his head and drew in a deep breath, not releasing his hold on her. Her eyes opened, and his heart beat wildly as he saw desire reflected in them. There was no sorrow there now, only passion that matched his own.

"I . . ." she started to say, then took a steadying breath. "I tell myself that this won't, can't, happen again, then the next thing I know, I'm kissing you. I shouldn't be doing this, Nick. It's confusing me, muddling my mind at a time when I have to be clear-headed to plan for the future. Emma and I are going to have to leave Serenity Cove, and I don't know where I should go."

"We'll study your options," he said, and kissed her nose. "I like your freckles. Why aren't they lined up in a neat row? For someone who's as organized as you are, you did a lousy job arranging your freckles."

"I have to tell Grandma and Grandpa Pauling that the cabins won't stand up under another winter," she went on. "Tonight. I'll tell them tonight."

"I'll go with you to tell them," he said, then trailed nibbling little kisses down the side of her neck.

Her knees weakened. "I can't think when you do that," she protested faintly.

"Don't think. Not now. Think later."

"But—"

"Think later, Pippa," he murmured, his mouth on hers again. "Kiss me. I checked your schedule, and kissing me is the next thing on your list of things to do."

"Well, then . . ."

"Right."

He kissed her hard, hungrily. Their tongues met, and passion burst into a raging flame that threatened to consume them.

Kissing Pippa, Nick thought hazily, was heaven. But, oh, Lord, he wanted more. He burned with desire for her, ached to be one with her, his manhood sheathed in the dark, sweet haven of her body. Their joining would be a celebration, more wondrous than anything he'd ever known. Pippa would be his, and he would be hers, one entity.

A soft purr came from her throat, and he echoed it with a rumbly groan. Her breasts were crushed to his chest, and he envisioned them bare, filling his palms before he drew first one, then the other, into his mouth. He would taste her, savor her, as his hands caressed all of her silken skin. He wanted this woman. Now.

Pippa couldn't think; she could only feel. Tingling sensations and driving heat were obliterating rational thought. There was nothing of importance beyond this man, beyond the urgent need he was creating within her. She wanted him to make love to her. Now.

"I want you, Pippa," Nick said, his voice raspy. "I want you so damn much. We're going to be sensational together, like nothing either of us has ever experienced before. There's just the two of us, you and me. Nothing else matters."

An icy hand seemed to clutch Pippa's heart, dousing the flame of passion within her, clearing her mind of the heat of desire. She sighed, a sad, weary sigh, and shook her head. She slid her hands down to rest on Nick's chest and met his smoldering gaze.

"Everything else matters," she said softly. "It isn't going to go away, don't you see? What's beyond that door is waiting for me. Just me. Not us. Nick, I haven't been with a man since Bill. If you and I made love it would be so . . . important, so consuming. I don't have anywhere to put something of that magnitude. There are too many things pulling at me, too many decisions that have to be made. Sometimes I feel as though I can hardly breathe because everything is crushing me. I can't deal with any more right now."

"Pippa—"

"No, listen to me. I want you, Nick. I can't deny that, but this isn't the time. I'm so afraid I would be using you to escape from my own reality. That would be wrong. Strange things happen to me when I'm with you. I don't behave like myself, and I don't know why. But I don't have the energy to try to figure out what this is between us. I have too many other things that I have to deal with, and they won't wait. I hope this makes sense. I'm so confused."

He cupped her face in his hands. "I understand. But you're forgetting something, Pippa. You have a friend now. Me. We'll sift through your problems one at a time, solve that one and go on to the next. I'll be right by your side through it all."

"Why?"

"Because that's where I want, where I need, to be."

"But why?"

"I'm not sure, but I can't find out unless I'm here. Yes, I want to make love with you, but I'll wait until the time is right. I'm confused about some things, too, Pippa. I need some answers and I intend to get them."

"You'd be better off going fishing and forgetting you ever met me," she said, shaking her head.

He smiled and stepped back from her. "Not a chance. Besides, I don't know how to fish. I grew up in Houston with the huge Capoletti clan. We were on the go all the time, in and out of trouble, but we never went fishing. I don't think any of my brothers, sisters, or cousins could sit still that long."

"I always wanted to be part of a large family. I can remember fantasizing about that when I was small."

"Pippa, where is your family?"

"I've got to go. Emma is over at the store with Grandma, and it's time for lunch. Thank you for letting me pour out my woes to you. I think . . . I know I'm going to like having you as a friend."

He brushed his thumb over her lips and smiled gently at her. "Good. It's a great place to start. Do be aware, however, that I intend to keep on kissing you every chance I get. As for making love, I'll wait. I'll give the cold-shower routine a shot. Pippa, think about my going with you to tell the Paulings what the financial situation is here at Serenity Cove. I know it's private, family business, but sometimes a fresh voice, another viewpoint, helps."

"Thank you. I'll think about it." She started toward the door. "Oh, I've got to put the ladder away."

"I'll do it. Where does it go?"

"No, I'll—"

"Pippa, I'll do it. You've got to get used to the idea that I'm here and willing to help you."

She opened the door and turned to look at him. "The ladder goes in the shed behind the store."

He nodded. "Fine."

"Well, I'm not going to make a big hoopla over a ladder."

"Good. Since that's settled, you ought to have a little space in your thoughts for something else."

"Such as?"

"Us," he said in a husky voice. "And the magic."

She gazed at him for a long moment, then left, closing the door softly behind her.

"Piece by puzzle piece, Peaches," Nick said. "One step at a time."

After eating three peanut butter and jelly sandwiches and drinking two tall glasses of milk, Nick filled out the registration card Pippa had given him and shoved it into the back pocket of his jeans. After putting the ladder away, he decided the red licorice was calling his name. When he entered the store he saw Grandma Pauling chatting with a young couple. He waved and wandered around, once more fascinated by the quaint establishment.

"Hello, there."

Nick turned to see a small, thin, nearly bald man smiling at him. The man was seventy-five if he was a day, Nick deduced. This had to be Grandpa.

"Hi," Nick said, extending his hand. "Nick Capoletti."

"Grandpa Pauling. Welcome to Serenity Cove. I've heard about you."

Nick laughed. "That sounds a bit ominous." He pulled the card from his pocket and attempted to smooth the bent corners. "I'm supposed to give this to Grandma."

"I'll take it," Grandpa said. "Did I just see you putting the ladder in the shed?"

"Yeah, I told Pippa I'd take care of it. Did I put it in the wrong place?"

"Oh, no, no. I was just wondering if Pippa was still tied to the chair you must have roped her to in order to have convinced her you were putting that ladder away."

Nick laughed. "You know her well. Actually, she didn't hassle me much about the ladder. We did go a few rounds when I found her crawling on the roof, though."

"Lordy, boy, I hope you didn't go on the roof, considering the size of you. No, you couldn't have, or you'd have fallen clean through."

Nick couldn't hide his surprise. "You know the roofs are in lousy shape?"

Grandpa glanced around, then whispered, "The whole place is falling apart. I'm only telling you this because Grandma says you're a fine fella, and you're sort of . . . well, looking after Pippa a bit. Nick, Serenity Cove is breathing its last breath. I'm not standing quietly by much longer watching Pippa work herself to a frazzle trying to save it. She's going to have to face the truth."

Nick opened his mouth, closed it, then shook his head before trying to speak. "Grandpa, this is going to sound like a cliché, but you folks have a communication problem here."

Grandpa squinted at him. "Beg your pardon?"

Nick raised a hand. "No, it's not my place to . . . Look, Pippa is planning on talking to you and Grandma tonight about—Well, I told Pippa I'd tag along. I think it would be best to wait until then to discuss all this."

"You've lost me, boy, but that's nothing new. I get confused at times, discussing the weather. The old mind just isn't as quick as it used to be. Now, there was a time when . . . Well, you don't want to hear about all that. Pippa did say Grandma and me was to come over about seven tonight for dessert. You'll be there?"

"I'll be there."

"Good enough. Glad you're here, Nick, mighty glad."

"Thank you, sir."

Nick left the store without his red licorice, deciding to avoid a conversation with Grandma Pauling. Shoving his hands into the back pockets of his jeans, he walked down the first trail he came to, deep in thought.

This was crazy, he mused. Pippa was trying to keep the true circumstances about Serenity Cove from Grandma and Grandpa Pauling, and they were attempting to hide the truth from her. That was really nuts.

The trail led to a cabin that wasn't his, so he retraced his steps and started over, going in another direction.

No, not nuts, he thought, reconsidering. These were people who cared deeply about one another, and wanted to protect one another. They were a family. Well, the Pauling family members had better lay their cards on the table, pronto.

He knew he had no business at the family gathering that evening. So said one part of his mind. But the other part insisted he had to be there. Pippa was in trouble. He needed to be there for her, show her that he cared, that she wasn't alone. Sure, Grandma and Grandpa Pauling loved her, but she was all mixed up about who was protecting whom from what. He was going to that meeting whether it would be considered charming of him or not.

Much to his surprise, the path he was on led him to an open, grassy area that sloped down to the lake. The lake appeared to be about half a mile across and a mile long. Two rowboats bobbed on it, and he could see the people in them holding fishing poles. Thunder rumbled in the distance, and he immediately decided he was glad he was on solid land, rather than in one of the boats. He continued on down to the lake, and saw Emma sitting under a tree, playing with a doll.

He hunkered down beside her. "Hi."

"Hi, Nick," she said, smiling at him.

She was really pretty, he thought. A miniature Pippa. Bill Pauling was the jerk of the decade to have walked out on Pippa and the coming baby who had turned out to be this enchanting little girl. It would really be something to come home at night to Pippa and Emma, to walk in the door and see their faces light up just because he was there. That was love, and that was family, and that was what had been missing from his life.

He had a large extended family, with many nieces and nephews, but that wasn't the same. He was once removed from it all, left alone while the others returned to their homes in pairs, with children as an added bonus. He'd felt a twinge—hell, a yank—of envy when Jared had married Tabor. They'd glowed with happiness. Then he'd gone to see Alison and Tucker, and watching them with their new son had brought a lump to his throat more than once.

Was it his turn? he wondered. Was what he was feeling for Pippa the beginning of the real thing, of a forever love? Was he really falling in love with Pippa Pauling? He had to find out. Because if Pippa and Emma were the stepping-stones to his future happiness, he had no intention of losing them.

"How come you're staring at me?" Emma asked.

"What? Oh, because you're so pretty, you just knock me over. Would you mind if I sat next to you here?"

"Well, I'm not supposed to talk to strangers, but I

guess I know you 'cause I saw you in your blue undies and stuff."

He chuckled as he sat down, leaning against the tree. He stretched out his legs and crossed them at the ankle.

"That's a nice doll you've got there," he said. "What's her name?"

"Ben."

"Ben. Well, that's an . . . interesting name for a little girl doll."

Emma sighed dramatically. "Well, see, I asked my mommy for a baby brother, but she said we couldn't have one 'cause we don't have a daddy. So I named my dolly Ben, and I pretend she's my baby brother." She sighed again. "It's not as good as a baby brother, though."

"No," Nick said, smiling, "I suppose it isn't."

"I sure wish my mommy would get us a daddy. Beth Ann has a daddy, and he laughs a lot, real loud. Mommies give hugs and smell good, and daddies laugh a lot. That's how it works."

"No joke? You're really smart, Emma."

She nodded. "I'm going to get smarter, too, when I go to first grade. Know what?"

"What?" Chalk up the loss of one heart to Miss Emma Pauling, he thought. What a neat kid.

"My birthday is next week, and I'm going to be six. But know what? When I'm seven my teeth are going to fall out. Beth Ann's big sister is seven and her teeth fell out. Do you think that's yucky?"

"Oh, no, not at all. It's a slick deal, Emma. You get money from the tooth fairy, then you grow new teeth."

"Oh," she said thoughtfully. "I didn't know that."

"Didn't you ask your mom about it?"

"No, 'cause she's got so much to do, and . . . Well, I made her sad when she said we couldn't have a daddy and a baby brother. I stamped my foot and was naughty and stuff, 'cause I said please and everything, but she still said no. So I didn't ask her 'bout my teeth falling out 'cause I didn't know if she'd get sad again. I don't like it when my mommy's sad."

"I don't either," Nick said quietly.

"She smiles when she's sad, but her eyes look funny. I can tell 'cause I'm smart."

"You sure are, Miss Emma."

"Do you got a baby?"

"No. No baby, no wife."

"Do you get sad eyes 'cause you don't got any?"

"Yes, I think maybe I do."

"Well, don't stamp your foot, 'cause that just won't work. You got to do something else to get a baby, and a daddy and mommy. I don't know what, but being naughty isn't it."

"Thank you for telling me. I'll remember not to stamp my foot."

"That's good." Thunder rumbled again, and Emma jumped to her feet. "I got to go. When it thunders I got to lickety-split home. Grandpa says lickety-split. 'Bye, Nick." She took off at a run, holding Ben by one leg.

" 'Bye," Nick said. Oh, yes, she was a nifty little kid. Smart as a whip, too. Pippa had done a terrific job raising her. But then, Pippa gave her all to everything she did. Just as when she kissed him. Just as she would when they made love. And they would make love when the time was right. He'd simply have to be patient, and remember not to stamp his foot, because that wouldn't cut it with Pippa.

Thunder rolled across the sky, and he stood up. "Get your butt home, Capoletti," he said. "Lickety-split."

He made it back to his cabin moments before the heavens opened and rain poured down in sheets. He set a match to the kindling and logs in the fireplace and watched the flames leap upward in a warming orange glow.

Now, this could be a very romantic scenario, he thought. Rain on the roof, cozy fire in the hearth, sipping wine and nibbling on cheese and crackers. And nibbling on lips. Ah, he thought, Italians really did have a knack for romance. Except . . .

Nick glanced around the room.

The scene sure was missing something, he thought glumly, when a guy was standing there with no one to talk to but an African violet named Peaches. He wanted Pippa there, right away, snuggled close to him in front of the fire. But he could stamp his foot from there to Sunday, and Pippa Pauling still wouldn't materialize. Hell.

He retrieved a paperback book from his suitcase and settled onto the sofa. Pippa's image superimposed itself over the words on the page, though, making it impossible to read. He closed the book with a snort of disgust.

He did not want to sit there alone. He'd had nearly thirty-one years of being alone, on the outside edge of everything. He wanted to be in the center of the circle where the love was, the warmth, the magic that never faded. He wanted to be there with Pippa.

A sudden pounding on the front door had him jerking in surprise; then he hurried to the door and flung it open.

"Pippa! What—"

"Nick," she said, gasping for breath. She was soaking wet, her hair was plastered down, and her eyes were wide and filled with fear. "The young honeymoon couple was fishing. They didn't pay attention to the thunder and . . . Oh, God, Nick, their boat overturned and they're out there on the lake, clinging to it. I don't know what to do!"

"Stay here," he said. He pulled the door closed and took off at full speed in the direction of the lake.

Pippa was right behind him.

Nick covered the distance quickly as mud splashed over him and the cold rain beat down. When he reached the edge of the lake he squinted through the downpour. He could barely make out the couple holding onto the overturned boat. Pippa reached his side, gulping in breaths of air.

"I told you to stay put," he yelled over the noise of the storm.

"I couldn't. They need help."

"Damn." He strode to one of the other boats and began to push it toward the water.

"What are you going to do?" Pippa hollered, following him.

"Go get them."

"I'll go with you."

He spun around and gripped her shoulders. "You stay right here, do you hear me? You're not going out on that lake, Pippa."

"But—"

"No! It's dangerous out there. I can't be worried about you *and* them. You have no right to put yourself at risk. Think about Emma, for God's sake. And, dammit, Pippa, think about me. I'm falling in love with you! And I'm sure as hell not going to let anything happen to you. Don't you move one inch!"

He released her and pushed the boat into the water, then jumped in and grabbed the oars.

Pippa stared after him, her mouth open, her mind reeling. He what? He was falling in love with her? Oh, Lord, she couldn't think about that now. Nick was in danger; those people were in danger. The lake was a wildly swirling demon.

She pressed trembling fingers to her lips, oblivious to the biting-cold rain as she watched Nick struggle with the oars.

Please, Nick, she silently begged. Please, be careful. He'd be all right. He was big and strong. He'd be all right. He'd reach the other two, pull them into the boat, and come back. He'd be all right. He would come back to her safe and sound.

Dear God, he just had to!

Four

Nick leaned forward, then tightened every muscle in his body, gathering his strength to pull back against the oars. The wind was whipping the rain and lake into a frenzy, and he struggled to steer his boat toward the barely discernible capsized one. Concentrating totally, he forced his body to perform to its maximum power, straining to the limit each time he drove the oars through the water.

I . . . Pull . . . love . . . Pull . . . Pippa . . . Pull . . .

The mental chant set his rhythm as he fought to overcome the fury of the storm. There was no time to examine his words, or the emotions rising within him. He had only one goal, one purpose, and that was to reach those two people before it was too late.

"Here!" a voice yelled. "Over here!"

Nick glanced over his shoulder, then maneuvered the boat farther to the right. Again he gathered his strength, tightened his quivering muscles, and shot the boat through the water. It thudded against the overturned one, and a young man pushed a woman toward him.

"She can't swim." The man gasped. "Can you pull her in?"

"Help me, help me," the young woman begged, sobbing.

"I'll pull, you push," Nick shouted. "Be careful. I don't want this one to tip over too."

"Okay," the man said. He turned to his wife. "Try to help. Ready? Up you go."

Pippa remained on the shore, unaware that she was trembling from head to toe with cold and fear. Her fingers were still pressed to her lips, her eyes wide, as she stared at the two boats. Her mind was a blur of panic, and she could no longer think. She could only see, could only feel the paralyzing fear that gripped her.

Two men came running down the slope to where she stood.

"We heard there was trouble," one said.

"Look out there," the other said, pointing to the lake.

"He's got them," the first said. "Lord, he's strong, pulling them out of the water like that. He's got them, though. The other guy is helping row back." He looked at Pippa. "Mrs. Pauling, are you okay? It's almost over. They'll be here in a few minutes."

Pippa turned her head to look at the two men. Dimly, she realized they were the occupants of cabin four.

"What?" she said.

"Everything is all right," the man said, smiling at her. "Whoever that guy is, he did a great job rescuing those two."

Pippa blinked. "Nick? Where . . ." She looked at the lake again. "Oh! They're almost here. Oh, thank God."

Grandpa Pauling came hurrying down the incline, wearing a bright yellow slicker. "Pippa!" he called, trying to catch his breath. "What's happening?"

"Nick has them, Grandpa. Nick has them."

"Praise the Lord," Grandpa said. "This storm came up fast and mean. Nick must have had a helluva time getting out there. We're lucky he was here."

"Jack," one of the men said, "come on. Let's get ready to pull that boat up onto land."

"Yeah."

As the rowboat neared the shore, the two men waded into the lake and grabbed the gunwale. Nick and the young man lunged against the oars once more, and the boat was suddenly out of the water and on land. The young man jumped out and reached for his sobbing wife.

"Thank you," he said to Nick. "Hell, that isn't good enough, but . . ."

Nick nodded, unable to speak as he dragged air into his burning lungs.

"That was something," Jack said to Nick. "Can you move?"

Nick stumbled out of the boat and sank to his knees as his legs refused to hold him. His muscles trembled and cramped, and he continued to draw in great gulps of air.

"Nick!" Pippa yelled. She ran to him and dropped to her knees. "Nick, are you all right? Nick?"

He nodded, then raised one hand, gesturing for her to wait until he could speak.

"We'll get these two to their cabin, Grandpa," Jack said.

"Good, good," Grandpa said. "Thanks for your help." He hurried to Pippa and Nick. "Nick, boy, are you with us?"

"Yeah," Nick said. "Damn. That was . . . some work-out."

Pippa threw her arms around his neck. "I was so frightened, so afraid something was going to happen to you. Are you sure you're all right?"

"He's breathing and talking, Pippa," Grandpa said, chuckling. "That's a real good sign that he's alive."

"Maybe," Nick said, staggering to his feet. Pippa wrapped her arms around his waist and looked up at him anxiously. "Yeah, I guess I'm alive after all."

"We're grateful to you, Nick," Grandpa said. "You saved those two kids. You'd think they'd have had enough sense to come in out of the rain. Pippa, we'll keep Emma with us. You and Nick go get warm and dry. Best take some aspirin, Nick. Every muscle in your body is going to be complaining about what you just did."

"Tell me about it," Nick said with a groan. "Oh, Lord."

"Go on with you, now," Grandpa said.

"Just don't ask me to go lickety-split."

Grandpa laughed. "Tend to our hero, Pippa," he said as he started back toward the path. "Emma is safe and sound with me and Grandma."

"Can you walk?" Pippa asked Nick, her arms still around his waist.

He smiled down at her. "If I say no, are you going to carry me?"

"Don't be silly. We'll just stay here until you *can* walk."

"Forget that. I'm freezing to death as it is. Are you sure this is Arizona?"

"Let's go." They started forward, and Nick circled Pippa's shoulders with one arm. She kept one of her own arms firmly around his waist. "You were wonderful, Nick. I was so frightened. I came to check on the boats and saw that the couple had capsized. I didn't even think—I just ran straight to your cabin."

"I'm glad you did," he said. "It means you're getting the message that I'm here for you, that you're not alone. You're a quick study, kid." He grinned at her. "You look like a drowned rat, but keep it up and you'll be as smart as Emma one of these days."

"You're starting to feel better. I can tell."

"Yeah. I'm okay," he said, as they sloshed through the mud. "I've felt like this after playing football, but I'm older now. I will most definitely take those aspirin. My muscles are like limp spaghetti. I'll take a warm shower, get into dry clothes, pop a couple of aspirin, and be as good as new. You need to shower and change, too, before you catch a cold. Tell you what. You go change, then come to my cabin. I'll build up the fire, fix us a hot toddy, then tell you forty-five times in a row that I love you."

Pippa stopped so abruptly that Nick staggered, causing a spray of muddy water to splash up to his knees.

"Oh, thanks," he said, "I needed that. What's a little more mud? Come on. This is no time to stop and admire the scenery."

"You don't love me," she said, staring at him.

"I most certainly do," he said indignantly. "I realize that screaming it in your face does not live up to my charming, romantic Italian image. Could we keep moving here?" He started walking again, propelling her forward by tightening his hold on her shoulders.

Pippa assumed her feet were plunking down one after the other, because she was keeping up with Nick. He loved her? He really was in love with her? No, that was crazy, totally insane. People didn't fall in love so fast. Did they? No, of course not. He really loved her?

Nick slid a glance at Pippa and smiled. He knew she was thinking about what he'd said, and the expression on her face announced she was shell-shocked. Well, she'd just have to get used to the idea. It had been clear as a bell when they'd stood by the lake and she had said she was going out in the boat with him. He'd known for certain that he loved her, no doubts, no maybes. And it felt good. There he was, slogging through the mud in the pouring rain, every muscle in his body aching, and he felt like a million bucks. Nick Capoletti was in love. He'd waited a long time for this, for love, for Pippa. Now he'd found her, and they would have the magic forever. Yes, Nick thought, it was good.

A frown drew his brows together as he realized he was getting a tad ahead of himself. There was the little matter of Pippa's not having said *she* loved *him*. Well, that was understandable. She had a lot on her mind. Serenity Cove was a disaster, and she was convinced she was going to break the senior Paulings' hearts with that news flash. Hey, she even had a kid whose teeth were going to start falling out in another year. Pippa had a lot on her plate, but he would help her sort it all through.

"Your abode, ma'am," he said, stopping in front of her cabin. "Do you have a slicker or umbrella?"

"Yes, but—"

"I'll be waiting for you at my place."

"But—"

"You heard Grandpa. You're supposed to tend to the hero. That's me. Lickety-split, kid." He dropped a fast, hard kiss on her lips, then strode away, splashing through the puddles.

"But—" Pippa said again, then threw up her hands and went into her cabin.

Nick stood under the beating water of the shower and swiveled his head back and forth with the hope of loosening the painfully bunched muscles in his shoulders. He'd set the temperature of the water as hot as he could tolerate it, and the bathroom was cloudy with steam.

Oh, Lord, he thought, groaning inwardly, his poor body was screaming for mercy. The heroes in the movies never suffered from their daring deeds. They did their thing, won the heart of the lovely lady, and rode off into the sunset. He would be doing well if he walked, let alone rode off anywhere. And there wasn't going to be a sunset, because it was raining buckets. But if he won the heart of the lovely lady, he'd be satisfied.

Beautiful Pippa was his lady, and he loved her. The question was, how did Pippa feel about him? Under the pile of her mounting problems, was she, too, slowly but surely falling in love?

She wanted to make love with him. She'd admitted that. She knew there was something special happening between them, but said she didn't have the mental energy to figure out what it was. That was the good news.

The bad news was, until Pippa's life and dilemmas got squared away, until she calmed down and wasn't walking around bone-weary, any feelings for him would take last place, buried beneath the rubble of her woes.

He turned off the water and quickly dried off. He had the picture now, he decided as he pulled on a clean pair of jeans. Well, not all of it. There were still pieces missing from the puzzle called Pippa. She wouldn't talk about her family, and he sensed something was very wrong there. She also seemed to have a nearly frantic need for order in her and Emma's life. She spoke often of stability and permanence, the importance of set patterns. A quirk in her personality? He didn't think so. There had to be more to it than that.

He pulled on a lightweight pale blue sweater, combed his hair, then went into the living room to stoke the fire. It was just burning nicely when he heard a knock at the door. He opened it to find Pippa standing on the porch clad in a bright orange slicker with a hood that fell to her eyebrows.

"Come in," he said. "You look like one of the seven dwarfs." She wasn't smiling. Her eyes were big and round, and she wasn't smiling. "Take that thing off and sit by the fire. Would you like a drink? Hot toddy? Hot chocolate?"

"No, thank you. I brought you some aspirin." She held out a bottle to him. "I wasn't sure if you had any."

He took the bottle. "Thank you. You're dripping on the floor, Pippa. Don't you think you should take that slicker off?"

She nodded and unsnapped it, then allowed him to draw it down her arms. He hung it on a peg by the door, as his gaze slid over her. She, too, was wearing jeans, and her green sweater matched her eyes perfectly. It also molded enticingly to her breasts. Her hair was damp, a wild disarray that beckoned to his fingers to weave through it.

"Let's sit in front of the fire," he said. He crossed the room, sat down on the sofa, and patted the cushion next to him. "Coming?"

She followed slowly and perched on the edge of the sofa, her hands clasped tightly in her lap, her gaze fixed on the fire.

Wonderful, Nick thought. There was nothing better than sitting next to someone who was stiff as a pencil. Pippa Pauling was very, very tense.

He set the aspirin bottle on the end table and stretched his arms out along the top of the sofa, being very careful not to touch Pippa. There was about a foot of sofa cushion between them, but it might as well have been a mile, he thought. Well, he'd better jump right in and find out what was wrong.

"What's wrong, Pippa?" he asked quietly.

She continued to stare at the fire. "Everything."

"Oh, is that all?" He smiled, but his smile faded when her expression remained bleak. "Look, could you give me a hint? You know, sort of start at the top of the everything list?"

She shifted her gaze to her tightly entwined fingers. "You said you love me."

"Yep. You can take that all the way to the bank. It hit me fast and hard, and it's the greatest thing that's ever happened to me. I've waited a long time for this, for you, and now I've found you. You believe that I'm sincere, don't you?"

"Yes. I thought about it while I was showering and

changing, and I realized that love does happen very quickly sometimes. Yes, I believe you."

"Well, good. Great. That's a step in the right direction." He resisted the urge to weave his fingers through her dark hair. "And the fact that I love you, Pippa, means that you're no longer alone. Whatever is troubling you, we'll face it together. I know you're upset about Serenity Cove, but the truth of the matter is`. . ." Hold it, Capoletti, he told himself. It wasn't his place to tell her what Grandpa Pauling had said. All that would be covered at the meeting tonight. ". . . these things have a way of working themselves out."

"The fact that Serenity Cove has to be sold isn't going to change."

"No, but—"

"That isn't what's on the top of the everything list at the moment," she said abruptly.

"Oh? Then what—Pippa, do you think you could look at me? I'd feel as though we were communicating a little better if I weren't talking to the side of your head."

She slowly turned to meet his gaze, and Nick slumped back against the arm of the sofa.

Talking to the side of her head was a lot safer, he thought. He wanted to lean toward her, capture her mouth with his, and kiss her until they couldn't breathe. But this wasn't the time, and he knew it. Her eyes were so big, and she looked so stricken, as though something had frightened her. He'd fix it, by damn. Whatever had her this upset, he'd fix it.

"That's better," he said, smiling at her. "Now, whip it on me. What's on the top of your everything-is-wrong list?"

"You."

He blinked in surprise. "Me? What did I do? I'm just the charming Italian who's in love with you."

"I know. But Nick, I told you I realized something was happening between us. Then I explained that I just couldn't deal with it right now. I didn't have the emotional energy to figure it all out, and I was also afraid I'd get so mixed up that I'd use you to escape from what I have to face. You said you understood."

"I do," he said, nodding. "It wasn't the greatest news I'd ever had, but I do understand."

"Nick, when we were at the lake, and you were out there in that boat, I was so afraid. I've never felt such fear. I kept thinking that I couldn't bear it if something happened to you. Somewhere in the middle of all that, I realized how very important you are to me."

"Hey, that's fantastic."

"No, it's not."

He leaned toward her. "Why not?"

"Because there's a possibility that maybe . . . That is, it could be that maybe . . . I don't know for sure, but maybe . . ."

"Pippa!"

"That maybe I'm falling in love with you," she said in a rush.

A big smile split his face. "That's—"

"Terrible."

The big smile slid right off his chin. "Sure sounded good to me. I'm in love with you, you're creeping up on falling in love with me, the hero gets the girl, and they ride off into the sunset. It's right on the mark."

"No, no, no," she said, shaking her head. "I can't ride off into the sunset with anyone. I have responsibilities, Nick. I have Emma and—"

He raised a hand. "Whoa. Hold it right there. Pippa, maybe I'm not making myself clear here. When we ride off into the sunset, we go as a family. You, me, Emma, and Ben."

"Ben?"

"Oh, well, he'll come later. He's the baby brother we're going to make for Emma. Pippa, I love you, I want to marry you. I've never been a husband before, but I'll work very hard at it. And I'm going to be a good father. Emma is a nifty kid, and I think she likes me. Damn, I wanted to propose to you in a romantic setting with candlelight and champagne. I'm really shooting my romatic-Italian image to hell, but . . . I'm asking you to marry me, to be my wife. Will you? Will you marry me, Pippa?"

Tears misted her eyes, and her voice trembled when she spoke. "No. I—I can't."

He reached over to stroke her face. "Pippa, don't say that. I believe that you do love me. I believe that if you stopped long enough to get in touch with yourself, really listened to your heart, you'd realize there isn't any maybe about it. The future is ours, together. You, me, Emma, the children you and I will create with our love. Don't say no to all that, to what we can share."

"I *have* to say no."

"Why? Pippa, do you love me?"

"I . . ." Tears spilled onto her cheeks. "Yes. When I was standing by the lake I knew that I loved you. But I can't marry you."

"Why the hell not?" Nick yelled. "No, erase that. Forget I yelled. I didn't yell." He took a deep breath and let it out slowly. "I'm calm, cool, and under control. Now, slow and easy. Pippa, why can't you marry me?"

"Because . . ." She swallowed past her tears. "Because I would never know if I was capable of taking care of myself and Emma on my own."

"You don't have to think about that. I'm going to provide for and protect both of you. I make good money. You'd never lack for anything."

"I don't even know what you do for a living in Las Vegas."

"I—"

"No, no, it isn't important. It's not the point. Nick, please listen to me. After Emma was born we barely scraped by. If the Paulings hadn't shown up when they did, I don't know what would have become of me and my baby. Grandpa and Grandma provided a home for us, security. Serenity Cove has been my haven, my safe place. I've been able to raise my child in the manner I'd hoped to, given her a stable, secure life. Now, that's all going to end."

"Yes, Serenity Cove has to be sold. The Paulings will decide on a new place to live, and you and Emma will come with me to Vegas. What's wrong with that?"

"Everything!"

"Here we go again." He shook his head. "Everything is wrong."

"Oh, no, not everything," she said, placing her hand on his arm. "Knowing that you love me, really love me, is wonderful. I've known for many years that I never loved Bill. I thought he was a way for me to have a real home, a place that would always be there. I convinced myself that I loved him and that he loved me. It just wasn't true. Now, I'm a woman, not a child. A woman that a magnificent man has fallen in love with, and I love you, Nick. I didn't think this would ever happen to me."

"Well, it has," he said gently, "so let's grab it and run."

"No. I said I'm a woman, but that isn't entirely true. I have to know that I'm capable of standing on my own two feet, taking care of myself and my child. The one time I tried to do that I failed."

"You were a kid," Nick said, his voice rising again.

"Who was rescued by the Paulings. Now they're going to move on, and . . . and what? I'm placed in your hands for safekeeping? You'll take care of me and Emma now because, after all, I'm not capable of doing it myself? No, Nick, I can't do it that way. I have to know I'm really a grown woman, don't you see that? If I'm to be your wife, I want to be your equal partner. We will provide for and protect our children together. I can't be just another one of your responsibilities."

"And what am I supposed to do in the meantime?" he asked loudly. "Twiddle my thumbs? Sit around and talk to Peaches while you're off proving heaven only knows what to yourself? Dammit, Pippa, I've waited a lifetime for what we can have together. Now you're saying I should wait some more while you set up housekeeping, get a job, show everyone you can keep a roof over your head and food on the table. I don't give a tinker's damn if you can do all of that. *I'm* going to provide those things for you and Emma."

"Well, *I* give a tinker's damn if I can do it," Pippa said, jumping to her feet. "It's important to me to know I'm capable."

"Oh, hell." Nick reached up, gripped her waist, and pulled her onto his lap. Pippa gasped in surprise. With one hand on her cheek, he forced her to look at him. "I love you," he said, "and you love me. Concentrate on that for now."

"But—"

"Pippa, please, just be quiet."

His mouth pressed against hers, his tongue delving between her lips. Pippa stiffened, but in the next instant was lost to the wondrous sensations that swept through her. She lifted one arm to circle Nick's neck, answering his kiss with all the love inside her.

His hand trailed down her body, then slipped beneath her sweater. His fingers inched up over her silken skin until he found a breast. Her wispy bra was little barrier, and his thumb stroked the nipple to a hard peak. A sigh of pleasure whispered from her in a puff of air across his lips. He took a deep breath, then claimed her mouth again.

She loved him, he thought. The woman he loved was in love with him, and nothing was going to stand in the way of their future. Pippa was getting all off track, trying to head down a road where she didn't need to go, needlessly proving she was capable of taking care of herself and Emma. No, he wasn't going to run the risk of losing her, wasn't going to wait to have a life with her that would be perfect for them, and Emma too. Pippa and Emma were both going to be his. They would be Capolettis, and he would take care of them.

"Say it again," he murmured. "Tell me you love me."

"I do," she whispered. "I love you, Nick."

"I want you, Pippa. Your words of love are sweet music, but I want more. I want to make love with you. It will be our commitment to each other, a joining that says whatever we face, we do it together. We'll work everything out, you'll see. You're not alone, I'm not alone, not anymore. Our magic is forever."

"Oh, Nick, you make me think that maybe there is such a thing as magic."

"Believe it." He slid his hand from beneath her sweater. "I love you." His mouth sought hers in a searing kiss. "Let me love you. Now."

Yes? No? Yes? Pippa wondered frantically. She wanted this, she truly did. Her body was humming with desire, with heat that swirled deep within her. It wouldn't be wrong, because this was Nick, the man she loved. The man who loved her. Yes? No? Yes?

"Pippa?"

"Yes," she whispered. "Oh, yes, I want you too."

With a throaty groan, he kissed her again, then with her in his arms, stood up. He held his precious cargo tightly to his chest as he walked down the hall to his bedroom, sore muscles forgotten. The rain still beat against the roof, but it was no longer a threatening force. It was a serenade just for them.

He set her on her feet, then wove his fingers through her hair, looking directly into her eyes.

"Are you sure?" he asked.

"Yes."

"It's going to be wonderful. You're not frightened, are you?"

"No." She paused. "Maybe a little. No, not frightened. Nervous. I'm not very experienced, Nick. I realize I was married and gave birth to a child, but I really don't know very much about pleasing a man."

He smiled at her, warmth mingling with the desire radiating from his dark eyes.

"You are very rare and very special, my Pippa. Just remember the magic."

He kissed her so softly, so tenderly, that fresh tears

misted Pippa's eyes. As he removed her clothes, he kissed and caressed her until she was trembling with need. Then he swept back the blankets and lay her on the cool sheets.

"You're so lovely, so exquisite," he said, his heated gaze sweeping over her. "And mine."

"Yes."

He quickly shed his clothes, and her breath caught as she looked at him. Tall and dark, tightly muscled and fully aroused, this was Nick, her love, her magic. He stretched out next to her and kissed her, one of his hands seeking her breast. She met his tongue boldly with hers, then sighed as his lips left hers to suckle her breast. He drew the soft flesh deep into his mouth, his tongue flicking over the nipple.

"Oh, Nick," she whispered as a raging fire swept through her.

His hand swept lower as his mouth moved to her other breast. His fingers found her moist heat and she gasped, her muscles tautening. Then she relaxed and savored each new and glorious sensation.

"You want me," he murmured. "Your body is ready for me. Pippa, this is going to be so good."

"I know. Oh, Nick, please come to me now. I feel strange . . . on fire. I've never, ever felt like this before. I want you. I want you so much."

He kissed her, a hard, searing kiss, then moved over her, catching his weight on his arms. He gazed into her eyes and saw all he needed to know. The love, the desire, the trust were there.

"I love you," he said, his voice husky with passion.

"And I love you."

He entered her slowly, carefully, waiting for her body

to adjust to him before he moved deeper into her silken heat. She received all of him, sheathing him, welcoming him.

"Oh, Pippa."

Slowly, and then more quickly, he moved inside her, thrusting even deeper as she lifted her hips to meet him. He wanted to take his time, wanted the pleasure to last for both of them, but it was too wonderful, too strong to resist. His control slipped from his grasp, and he plunged wildly inside her.

"Nick! Oh, Nick, yes!"

"Oh, Pippa," he said, gasping. "Come with me, Pippa. This is the magic."

She clung tightly to his sweat-slicked shoulders as she was flung into a paradise she'd never known before. She called to Nick, wanting him with her in that wondrous place. He thrust deeply within her one last time, then shuddered, her name a hoarse whisper on his lips as he joined her in the ecstasy, his strength spilling from him into her. He collapsed against her, and she wrapped her arms around him, feeling their hearts thundering together.

"Oh, Nick," she whispered. "I've never . . . I didn't know. It was beautiful. It was . . . magic."

He lifted his head and pushed himself to his forearms. "Yes. Oh, yes, it was. Thank you, Pippa, for giving of yourself so totally, so trustingly. Lord, how I love you."

He kissed her, then eased off her. Pulling her close to his side, he covered their cooling bodies with the blankets. She tangled her fingers in the dark, moist hair on his chest, her eyes half-closed in sated contentment. Neither spoke. Words weren't needed. Their thoughts were as meshed as their bodies had been while each cherished the joy they had shared.

Time lost meaning. The rain quieted even more, falling with a gentle touch that lulled Pippa to sleep, her hand resting on Nick's chest.

He gazed down at her, sifting through her hair with his fingers as he smiled. It was chilling to think he might have gone a lifetime without discovering Pippa, and love. But he *had* found her, and he was never going to let her go.

She stirred, and her hand slid lower on his body. He sucked in his breath as desire rocketed through him, then firmly told himself he was not going to kiss Pippa awake and make love to her again. It had been many years since she'd been with a man, and she'd need some time to recuperate. He'd think about something other than where Pippa's hand was.

He frowned. Pippa had refused to marry him. Now, there was a depressing topic he could concentrate on. The woman he loved refused to marry him. She loved him, but wanted to prove to herself that she could take proper care of and provide for herself and Emma.

His frown deepened. Any way he looked at it, Pippa's stand on the issue was nuts. *He* was going to take care of his family. If Pippa wanted to work outside the house, fine, dandy, no problem. But she didn't have to make a crusade out of it, refuse to marry him until she'd passed some kind of test she'd set up for herself. Yes, it was nuts. And somehow he had to convince her it was nuts, without setting off her temper.

Her hand shifted again, and all thought fled Nick's mind except for the pulsing awareness of his desire for her. He kissed her lightly on the forehead. The nose.

He slid the tip of his tongue along her bottom lip. Nothing. Pippa slept on.

"Well, damn," he muttered.

A tiny bubble of laughter bounced through the air.

"Hey, you're awake. You wicked woman. Those busy fingers of yours have been driving me crazy, and you knew it."

She opened her eyes, merriment sparkling in them. "Me?"

"Yes, you. Now you'll pay the price."

"No," she said, her busy fingers becoming even busier. "Now I will reap the rewards."

Five

At seven that evening, Nick stepped up onto the porch of cabin one. The rain had stopped, leaving the air clean and crisp. The beginning of a vibrant sunset could be seen peeking through the tops of the tall pines.

He hesitated before knocking, as memories of his exquisite lovemaking with Pippa tumbled through his mind. He saw again every inch of her lissome body, the satiated smile on her face, her hair tumbled in sensual disarray over the pillow. Never before had he shared such completeness, such ecstasy and splendor, as when he'd become one with Pippa.

It was the difference, he knew, between having sex and making love. There was no comparison with anything he'd experienced in the past. Nothing could equal what he'd felt with Pippa. It had been a joining not only of bodies, but of hearts, souls, minds. He was in awe of this emotion named love, and treasured the knowledge that at last it was his. Pippa was his.

They just had a few things to work out.

He knocked on the door, and Emma flung it open. "Hi, Nick. We're having gingerbread with whipped cream." She stepped back so he could enter. "My birthday cake is going to be chocolate with chocolate frosting and six candles to blow out."

He smiled at her as she shut the door behind him. "You should be thinking of a special wish to make when you blow out those candles."

"I know my wish," she whispered. "I'm gonna wish for a baby brother and a daddy."

Nick's heart did the two-step for a moment. "That's a super wish, sweetheart. Perfect."

"Good evening, Nick," Grandpa said, rising from a chair by the fire. "How are you feeling after your ordeal on the lake?"

"Fine," Nick said, walking forward to shake Grandpa's hand. "No worse for wear. A hot shower fixed me right up." And what had taken place in his bed with Pippa hadn't been too shabby, either. He felt like *two* million bucks. "Are those two all right?"

"Oh, yes, just shook up a bit. We all are very grateful for what you did."

"Indeed, we are," Grandma said, appearing in the doorway to the kitchen. "Very grateful."

"I'm glad I could help," Nick said.

Grandma stepped into the room. "Life is strange at times, isn't it? It seems that a great deal depends on being in the right place at the right time, then knowing what to do when you get there."

Oh, that crafty Grandma, Nick thought, smiling. She was talking about him and Pippa now.

"I thoroughly agree, Grandma," he said.

"Thought you might." She smiled, too, and settled into a rocker by the fire.

Nick glanced around and saw that Pippa's cabin had the same floor plan and decorating motif as his. There were personal touches, though, that said this was home, not a vacation retreat. Several framed pictures sat on the mantel, there was a covered candy dish on an end table, and a bookcase held knickknacks and paperback books. Not fancy, he thought, but charming, with an aura of permanence provided by Pippa's caring attention. She'd bring that warmth to the home they'd create together. But first, he had to get her off the top of this mountain.

"Hello, Nick."

His head snapped around, and he saw Pippa walking into the room. She stopped, their eyes met, and memories of the past hours flooded over them. Neither moved, and both could hardly breath. Heat gathered low in Nick's body. A flush crept onto Pippa's cheeks. The room faded into oblivion.

"Mommy, can we have gingerbread now?" Emma asked.

Nick jerked in surprise at the sound of Emma's voice. He cleared his throat and tore his gaze from Pippa's. Grandma laughed softly, but he decided not to look at her, fearing what might be written plainly on his face.

"What?" Pippa asked. She looked at Emma as though she'd never seen the little girl before in her life. "Oh! Yes, of course. It's all ready. Let's go into the kitchen."

Grandpa pulled a folded white card from his pocket. "I'll put Nick's registration card on your desk here, Pippa. It's a bit the worse for wear, I'm afraid."

"That's fine," Pippa said. "Everyone ready for gingerbread and whipped cream?"

The dessert was delicious, the conversation lively. As though by unspoken agreement, Pippa didn't look directly at Nick, and he didn't look directly at her. Since Grandma kept laughing softly even when nothing particularly humorous had been said, though, Nick wondered if anyone was fooled by his and Pippa's casual manner.

Pippa whisked Emma off at eight o'clock for a bath while Grandma, Grandpa, and Nick made quick work of the dishes. Emma reappeared in a long flannel nightie, her braids undone, so her shiny, freshly brushed, dark hair tumbled down her back. She hugged Grandma and Grandpa, then lifted her arms to Nick.

He dropped to one knee and wrapped his arms around her. "Holy mackerel, you smell good," he said. "There is nothing finer than the scent of soap, powder, and toothpaste."

She giggled and kissed him on the cheek. "Don't tell nobody 'bout my birthday wish," she whispered. "That will wreck it."

"My lips are sealed, sweet Emma." He kissed her on the forehead. "Sleep tight, and don't let the bedbugs bite."

She giggled again, then wiggled out of his arms, hiked up her nightie, and ran from the room.

Nick got to his feet. "Neat kid. She's a heartbreaker, that one."

"Pippa has done a wonderful job with her," Grandma said, hanging up the dish towel. "Our son is a fool. We're partially to blame for spoiling him, but there's no excuse for the way he deserted Pippa. Lord only knows where William is. None of us has heard from him in years."

"Don't upset yourself talking about William," Grandpa

said. "We have enough to deal with yet this evening. Let's go into the living room and wait for Pippa. We can't put off any longer what needs to be said about Serenity Cove."

Amen to that, Nick thought.

In the living room, he stood by the fire, leaning one forearm on the mantel. Grandma settled into the rocking chair again, and Grandpa sat on one end of the sofa.

Pippa came into the room. "Emma's all tucked in. Would anyone like more coffee?"

"No, Pippa," Grandpa said, "we're fine. Come sit down. We have to talk."

Pippa sat on the opposite end of the sofa. "Yes, I know. I need to talk to you and Grandma too." She took a deep breath and folded her hands in her lap. "It's about Serenity Cove."

Easy, Pippa, Nick thought. He could feel her tense up even from where he stood. She was in for a rush of relief when she found out that the Paulings already knew that Serenity Cove was finished.

"Being the oldest person in the room," Grandpa said, "I'm pulling rank and speaking first. Pippa, Grandma and I can no longer stand by and watch you work yourself to a frazzle trying to save Serenity Cove. We realize this is home to you, and we know how important a sense of permanence and stability is to you because of your childhood."

Nick stiffened. Childhood? The family she wouldn't speak of? He was missing those pieces of the puzzle that was Pippa. What about her childhood? Well, this obviously wasn't the time to ask.

"Knowing how you felt," Grandpa went on, "we kept still, but no more. You're going to have to face what

Grandma and I already know. It's time to sell Serenity Cove."

Pippa's eyes widened. "What?"

"Child," Grandma said gently, "it must be done. It's served us well, and we've all been happy here, but Serenity Cove is of another era. We can't compete with the resorts and all they offer. We're going to have to leave our mountain, but we'll do it with a sense of adventure, of anticipation of what is waiting for us elsewhere. We'll shed our tears, then say good-bye to Serenity Cove. It's time."

"But—" Pippa started to say.

"When Nick mentioned you'd been checking the roofs," Grandpa said, "I told him we couldn't stay on here, that everything was falling apart."

Pippa jumped up off the sofa. "You knew?" Her wide-eyed gaze swept over the three of them. "You all knew we couldn't go on? I've been sick with worry about the finances, was dreading the thought of having to tell you and maybe break your hearts, and you already knew? Even you, Nick? Grandpa told you this morning, but you never said a word to me? Why?"

"We were trying to protect your feelings," Grandpa said, "your sense of security. We put it off as long as we could. It can't be postponed any longer."

"Protect me?" Pippa repeated, her voice rising. "The way you'd protect a child?"

"Take it easy, Pippa," Nick said quietly. "Everyone did what they thought was best, you included. It's all out in the open now."

"A little after the fact, isn't it?" she said, narrowing her eyes. "I thought you were here tonight, Nick, to help me tell Grandma and Grandpa that Serenity Cove had to be sold. But you already knew they were very aware of that. You asked me to marry you knowing full well you weren't taking on the devastated senior Paulings. How very convenient for you, Mr. Capoletti."

"Hey, wait a minute," he said, pushing himself away from the mantel. "You're twisting this all around. It wasn't my place to tell you what Grandpa had said. I knew he'd tell you tonight and—"

"Yes, you knew," Pippa said, planting her hands on her hips. "All of you knew." She shook her head. "I can't believe this. Protecting me like a child. Now poor little Pippa is to be passed into Nick's care because she's lost her precious Serenity Cove. Nick will protect poor Pippa from the big bad world. Well, I am not a child! I'm a woman, and I really resent this. I'm perfectly capable of taking care of myself and Emma. Emma, as you all seem to have forgotten, is the child around here, not me."

"Oh, honey," Grandma said, "you're taking this all wrong. You were working so hard, and we never dreamed you were trying to hold things together for us. We thought you needed to be here as badly as you always had, and we hated telling you it was going to end soon."

"So Grandpa tells Nick, and Nick leaps to the rescue, hero that he is. You can leave here knowing Nick is going to protect me, take care of me now. Nick knows you're happy as clams, and he's only got me and Emma to worry about. How very neat and tidy for all of you."

Grandpa shook his head. "That's not how it happened, Pippa. You're seeing things that aren't there. We love you. From what has been said, Nick loves you too. We're all going to be fine. You're forgetting that you're loved, Pippa, very much."

She stared at him for a long moment, then drew in a

deep breath. "Yes, I know," she said softly. "I'm sorry. Grandma, Grandpa, I'm very sorry. There's no excuse for my behavior. I've been concerned about you, about Serenity Cove. There have been so many changes to face so quickly, it seems. I love you both, and I'm very grateful for all you've done for me and Emma. I apologize for accusing you of treating me like a child."

What a woman, Nick thought. He knew some people who'd turn blue before they apologized for anything they'd done. When he loved, his heart picked well. Pippa was really something.

Grandma got up from the rocker and walked over to Pippa. She hugged her tight, then held her at arm's length to look at her.

"We're the ones who are grateful that you and Emma have been with us all these years. Leaving Serenity Cove doesn't mean we're never to see each other again. Mercy, no. We're moving off our mountain, not to another planet."

"That's true," Grandpa said.

"As for treating you like a child," Grandma went on, "you're right, we did exactly that. We decided your need to be here was so great, we feared telling you the truth, protected you from it. You thought we were so old and feeble-minded, we couldn't see what was happening to Serenity Cove right under our noses. We surely gave that impression, and you were left with all the worry on your shoulders. We're the ones who should apologize, Pippa."

"Oh, Grandma, I love you so much," Pippa said. "You and Grandpa have been everything to Emma and me."

"And we'll always be there for you," Grandpa said, rising. "We all have plenty of time to make our plans. I'll call that real-estate agent who was so nice on her last visit, and have her come up tomorrow if she's free.

She said she had people interested in this property, but even so, it will be a while before we have to pack up and go."

Pippa nodded.

"I think we've all had enough for one day," Grandpa said. "Good night, Pippa. Come along, Grandma."

"Good night, dear," Grandma said, patting Pippa's cheek. "Good night, Nick."

"Good night," he said.

Pippa walked the Paulings to the door, then shut it behind them. She leaned back against it, closing her eyes.

Nick looked at her, waiting, not knowing what to do. He wanted to go to her, to hold her tightly and safely in his arms. He felt as though he were on thin ice that could crack beneath him at any moment. Pippa had included him in her list of those who were treating her like a child, yet had apologized only to Grandma and Grandpa after her angry tirade. What was she thinking now? Damn, the silence in the room weighed a ton.

"Pippa?" he said quietly.

She slowly opened her eyes and sighed. "That was quite a performance I put on."

"Everything is fine now, out in the open. You've been carrying too much on your shoulders for too long, and it caught up with you, that's all. I'm sure hearing that the Paulings already knew the truth was a shock, but it's over. It's time to look to the future."

"Yes, the future." She pushed herself away from the door and met his gaze. "I shouldn't have been angry at Grandma and Grandpa for treating me like a child, because in many ways I am one."

"That's not true, Pippa. You're a woman who has worked very hard here and done a terrific job. You're a single parent raising a wonderful little girl, which is no easy task. Don't sell yourself short."

"I'm facing the truth. It's long overdue, you know. There's the truth about having to leave here, and the truth about who I am—or rather, who I'm not."

"You're losing me," he said, shaking his head.

"Nick, I know nothing about the real world except for the few months I was alone years ago, and then I nearly got Emma and myself evicted from our apartment. It's been safe on this mountain, like a cocoon. Grandpa and Grandma have always been here for me, for Emma. I haven't raised her alone; I had help every day. I haven't grown up, not really, since the day I arrived here."

"Come on, Pippa, give yourself credit for having efficiently run a vacation retreat. People go to school to learn how to do that. You learned it, and did it, on your own. You have a marketable skill."

"Do I? I have to know that for sure. I have to know that I'm capable of taking care of myself and Emma."

An icy fist seemed to grab hold of Nick's heart, and his muscles tensed. "What are you saying?" He crossed the room and gripped her shoulders.

Pippa looked up at him. "I'm only repeating what I said before, Nick. I can't, won't, marry you until I know I'm a competent, complete woman who can stand alone. I need to know that. I *have* to know that."

He squeezed his eyes closed for a long moment, then looked at her again. "Pippa, I love you. I want to marry you now, start our life together. We're going to be a family. Don't put our future on hold."

"I love you, too, Nick, I swear I do. But please, please, try to understand that this is something I have to do. You have the option of—of choosing not to wait for me."

America's most popular, most compelling romance novels...

Here, at last...love stories that really involve you! Fresh, finely crafted novels with story lines so believable you'll feel you're actually living them! Characters you can relate to...exciting places to visit...unexpected plot twists...all in all, exciting romances that satisfy your mind and delight your heart.

Get one full-length Loveswept FREE every month!
Now you can be sure you'll never, ever miss a single
Loveswept title by enrolling in our special reader's home
delivery service. A service that will bring you all six new
Loveswept romances each month for the price of five—and
deliver them to you before they appear in the bookstores!

Examine 6 Loveswept Novels for

15 days FREE!

(SEE OTHER SIDE FOR DETAILS)

"Oh, yeah, right." He stepped back from her and dragged one hand through his hair. "Sure thing. I'll just push a button and turn off everything I feel for you. No problem. I can replace you just as I replaced the first Peaches the violet. Good Lord, Pippa, what kind of man do you think I am?"

"You're getting angry."

"Got it in one, kid. I'm mad as hell. I've waited a lifetime for love, and now here you are. And you love me. I don't feel like being understanding. I want what I want, and I want it right now. I also sound like a candidate for Emma's baby brother, because I think I'm throwing a tantrum."

She smiled, and he took a deep breath.

"Look, let's agree on a couple of things, okay?" he said. "This is obviously going to call for a great deal of patience and compromise. Lord, I hope I remember to be charming. Anyway, if you won't marry me now and live under the same roof with me, it seems only fair that you at least live in the same town. You could get a job and have your own apartment in Las Vegas. I'll . . . court you. Yes, there we go, that's a great word. Okay?"

"I don't know," she said slowly. "You'd be a phone call away if anything went wrong."

"Come on, Pippa, give me a break. You can't call all the shots. Compromise, remember?"

"Yes, you're right."

"Then you'll move to Vegas?"

"Yes."

"Good. Next up. Just how long do you need to prove to yourself what it is you're proving to yourself?"

"Nick, I can't answer that. It will be something I'll sense, feel, within me. I can't mark a date on the calendar and say, 'There, on that day I'll be a complete, capable woman.' That's impossible."

"Can't you give me a ballpark figure? A rough estimate of time?"

"No."

Nick's expletive was extremely earthy.

"That was *not* charming, Mr. Capoletti."

"Well, hell, I'm really hating this." He paused, then cradled her face in his hands. "That's enough heavy stuff for tonight. This has been one wingdinger of a day. And some of it"—he lowered his head toward hers— "was sensational."

"Oh, yes," she whispered before his lips claimed hers.

The kiss evoked memories of ecstasy shared, and brought promises of more to come. Nick dropped his arms to gather Pippa close, and she nestled her body against his.

"I want to make love to you," he murmured.

"I want you, too, but Emma—"

"—is asleep. Your hours as a mother are over for today. This is man-and-woman time. Me. You. Us."

She moved back enough to be able to look up at him, and she could see the raw desire in his dark eyes. She knew he could see the same need in her own eyes.

"Yes," she said softly, "you're right. These hours are ours."

He kissed her again, a soft, lingering kiss, which caused her knees to tremble and her heart to race. With his arm around her shoulders, they walked down the hall together to her bedroom. She closed the door and turned on the lamp by the bed, then moved back into his embrace.

"It's all going to work out, Pippa," he said quietly. "Step by step, one thing at a time."

"Everything's happening so quickly," she said, resting her head on his chest.

"I know, but as long as we remember that we love each other, we'll be fine."

"Nick, do you really understand why I need to prove to myself that I'm capable of caring for Emma and me?"

"Yes, I think I do. I come from such a big family that I have relatives from one end of Houston to the other. Whatever they did, good or bad, reflected on me. I felt a tremendous sense of relief when I moved to Vegas, because I knew I would be judged only for myself. I needed that, needed to know that if I succeeded, or fell flat on my face, I would have done it on my own."

"Yes, exactly. Then you *do* understand."

"I'm telling myself that I do, but it's tough, because I'm in love with you, and I want to start our life together. I'll try not to crowd you or rush you, Pippa, but waiting for you to marry me is going to be very difficult. I'll do the best I can."

"Thank you, Nick. I do love you so much. I want to be all I should be for you, and for myself." She paused. "Nick?"

"Hmm?"

"Could we quit talking now?"

He chuckled. "Most definitely, ma'am. We're shifting from our talking mode to our action mode."

"Oh, good."

"It's going to be better than good. This will be fantastic."

An eagerness engulfed them, and they quickly shed their clothes, wanting no barriers between them. Nick tossed back the blankets on the bed, and they tumbled onto the cool sheets, reaching for each other. They touched and kissed, caressed, tantalized, discovered. Where hands went, lips followed. Nothing was too bold; no secrets were kept. Hearts raced, and blood pounded in their veins like liquid fire.

When they could bear no more, they became one with a thundering cadence that swept them instantly up and away from reality. Holding each other, calling to each other, they cast themselves far beyond anyplace they had gone before. Wave after wave of exquisite sensations swept through them, finally quieting to tiny ripples before leaving them spent.

They lay close, entwined, savoring. Their world went no further than the one by their side. Their bodies cooled, their heartbeats returned to normal, the room came back into focus.

"Fantastic," Nick finally said.

"Yes."

"I didn't hurt you, did I? I was so rough with you."

"Oh, no, I'm fine. More than fine. I was rather rough myself."

He smiled. "You were sensational."

She laughed softly and snuggled closer to him. "You've created a monster, Capoletti."

"No," he said, weaving his fingers through her tumbled hair. "You're a woman who loves her man. It's as simple as that."

"And as complicated."

"Yeah, I suppose."

They lay in silence for several minutes, relishing the sated contentment they felt.

"Pippa," Nick said, "I hate to shatter this lovely mood, but don't you think it's time you told me about your parents, your family? I'm trying to piece it all together, and I get the distinct impression that your determination to have order in your life stems from something in your childhood. Would you share it with me?"

She sighed. Her fingers that had been fiddling with the curly hair on Nick's chest stilled. He waited, silently urging her to speak.

"My father was a banker," she said quietly. "He was very old-fashioned, believed in the teachings of his parents and his grandparents. The man was the provider, the woman the nurturer. He liked order in his life. Monday was wash day, Tuesday was baking day, that sort of thing. Every Sunday we had pot roast, potatoes, and cooked carrots. He read me a story at night at exactly the same time, walked in the door from work each day at exactly the same time, never varied his routine. I adored him. He wasn't stuffy or dull; he was simply a man who had to have order."

"I get the picture," Nick said. "And your mother?"

"I didn't realize it at the time, but she was terribly unhappy. She loved my father, but was bored. She felt trapped in an existence that didn't vary from one week to the next, one year to the next. She told me years later that she tried to explain her feelings to my father, but he said he was who he was. My mother's only act of rebellion was when she named me. Pippa Patterson. Pippa was a fun, whimsical, storybook name, she said, and held her ground until my father gave in. I hated my name. The kids at school teased me unmercifully."

"That's why you gave your daughter such an old-fashioned name."

"Yes. When I was nine, my father died of a heart attack. My world was shattered. Everything fell apart. Overnight, it seemed, my mother changed into someone I didn't know. She was well provided-for by my father's estate, and she didn't have to work. She became a crusader of causes, anything and everything. She picketed, took part in sit-ins, even spent a night in jail. I never knew how many people might be sleeping on the living-room floor when I got up in the morning. Our house was the gathering place for different groups. What had been order turned into chaos."

"Oh, Pippa, I'm sorry," Nick said, stroking her back.

"I hated it, Nick. I'd lost my father, and was suddenly in a frightening world. I'd come home from school to find a strange woman who'd volunteered to stay with me while my mother was off to heaven only knew where for days. Time passed and I just muddled through, feeling lost and lonely in my own house. When I was a teenager I spent more and more time at the library or the movies, anywhere but at home. My mother and I went weeks at a stretch without speaking, hardly seeing each other. She didn't come to my high-school graduation because she was in San Francisco, probably standing on a street corner handing out pamphlets about some cause."

"Good Lord," Nick muttered, his jaw tightening.

"I got a job as a waitress, then met Bill Pauling. Just as my father had, Bill worked in a bank—a nice, solid, real bank—I grabbed onto him like a lifeline, and he was flattered, I guess, that I wanted to spend all my free time with him. He was rather shy, didn't have many friends, and we filled the voids in each other's lives. When he asked me to marry him I didn't hesitate. I loved him, I told myself, and he and I would have a wonderful life together. The chaos would become order again. I'd see to it."

"But he left you."

"Yes. We just had a civil ceremony, with a couple of friends as witnesses, because I really didn't know where my mother was at the time. Then Bill quit his job at the bank. He told me he never stayed at one job long, because he got bored. He sold used cars next. I never knew when he was coming home. I'd make dinner, but he wouldn't show up. We argued about it, and he said he'd grown up at Serenity Cove with a list of chores he had to do every day. He hated the regimentation, the routine. He wanted every aspect of his life to be free of all that. Why he married me, I'll never know. I got pregnant, and he was furious at the idea of a baby restricting his freedom. So he left. You know the rest."

"What about your mother? Did she know by then that you were married? Didn't she realize you weren't living at home any longer?"

"She didn't care. Can you believe that, Nick? She didn't care!"

"Oh, Pippa, I don't know what to say to you. This is all so lousy."

"It was as though my mother had been playing a part in a play while my father was alive. The woman who emerged after his death was a stranger to me. What she was doing wasn't wrong, it was just so foreign to the way she had been. If I had been different, more like her, I could have fallen into the new lifestyle she created and been perfectly happy. But I couldn't do it. I needed the structure, the certainty, that had been there when my father was head of the house. I didn't find that again until the Paulings brought Emma and me here to Serenity Cove."

"Did you go to your mother when Bill left you?"

"Yes. I was terribly frightened, and wasn't feeling well. I went to the house, and all these people were milling around. My mother waved at me from across the room, and I realized she didn't consider me a part of her life any longer. I managed to get her alone in the kitchen and said I had to talk to her, that I needed her."

"And?"

"She patted my hand and said we'd have a fun girl-to-girl chat when she got back from Alaska. They were all going up there on a crusade to save the seals, or whales, or penguins. I don't know. I walked out of the house and never went back. I've had no contact with her since. There's no point in it. My mother and I are from different worlds. I'm not standing in judgment of her, I just don't have anything to say to her. We have nothing at all in common."

"Well, *I'm* standing in judgment of her," he said fiercely. "She deserted you, in her own way, as much as Bill Pauling did. Yes, she had the right to make a new life for herself after your father died, but not at the expense of her child's welfare. For crying out loud, Pippa, she was a mother before she was a crusader for penguins. She had no right to quit that role just because something that looked like more fun, that was more exciting, came along."

"Nick, please, getting upset about it now won't change anything. I tried to make a go of it on my own, but I failed. Thanks to Grandma and Grandpa, Emma and I have had a wonderful life here at Serenity Cove. I've been able to give Emma the same kind of structure and security my father gave me. She's a happy little girl, just as I was before my father died. It's the thought of disrupting her life by moving away that distresses me the most, but it can't be helped. I didn't want her life turned upside down like this. Not ever."

"This is different, Pippa. You'll still be with Emma through the whole thing. People move constantly in this country, and the kids do fine. Sure, she'll miss Grandma and Grandpa, but she can visit them, and they'll visit you. If you have an upbeat attitude about this, Emma will pick up her cues from you. There's no comparison to what your mother did to you."

"I hope Emma will be all right. This is the only world she's ever known. But, Nick, do you understand better now why I must make it on my own? I've never done it, not once."

"I think you're wrong. I think you were making it on your own from the day your father died, but I'll never convince you of that. You'll have the time you need, Pippa. I can only hope it doesn't take too long. Thank you for telling me all this."

"You had the right to know who I am."

"Pippa, structure, routine, schedules are all very well and good, but there should be room for surprises, spur-of-the-moment ideas when you just drop everything and go for it, have some fun."

"I suppose."

He leaned back to look down at her. "But do you ever do things like that?"

She smiled. "I'm in this bed with you right now, Mr. Capoletti. Does that count?"

He smiled too. "It definitely counts for a great deal, but I was speaking more along the lines of going on a picnic, or making a batch of popcorn at midnight for no other reason than because you're in the mood for popcorn."

"Well, no, I guess I don't do things like that. My days and evenings have been pretty well scheduled for years. So have Emma's. But that's important to a child, Nick. Believe me, it is."

"So are picnics." He lowered his head toward hers.

"Big folks and little folks should take time out for picnics, fun, surprises." He nibbled on her bottom lip. "Don't you like surprises, Pippa?"

She shivered from the sensuous onslaught of his mouth. "I—I haven't had many surprises."

His hand slid up to cup one of her breasts. "Well, we'll just have to see what we can do about that."

"Mmm," she murmured as desire swept through her.

Nick's mouth melted over hers, and thought fled. There were only taste, feel, heat, and want. Then ecstasy once again as they flew beyond reality to a special place known only to themselves.

Two hours later, Nick entered the kitchen of his own cabin and took a beer from the refrigerator. He wandered back into the living room and slouched down on the sofa, stretching his legs out toward the cold fireplace.

Strange, he thought. He'd never met Pippa's mother or Bill Pauling, but the actions of those two were having far-reaching effects on his life. Pippa's past was determining his future. Love was, indeed, very complicated.

He knew he had a rough road to go before Pippa would at last be his wife. He was going to have to muster up every ounce of patience he possessed as Pippa set about proving to herself she was a capable woman. Damn.

He sighed. He had no choice but to wait. The tricky part would be trying to stay charming while he was grinding his teeth in frustration. If he were calling the shots, he and Pippa would be married before his vacation at Serenity Cove was over. Well, at least he'd gotten her to agree to move to Vegas.

He took a deep swallow of beer. He was hating this again, really hating it. It would help a whole helluva lot if a man could go out and buy himself a bushel of patience.

He threw his empty beer can in the kitchen trash, then glanced at his violet.

"Got any spare patience I can borrow, Peaches?" he asked. "No, huh? Some pal you are."

He strode from the kitchen and, for lack of anything better to do, went to bed.

Six

Nick slept late the next morning, then took a long, hot shower to ease the muscles that had tightened during the night. The day was sunny and clear, the trees seeming to sparkle in the sunlight after the rain.

Dressed in navy blue shorts and a white knit shirt, Nick stepped out onto his porch, filled his lungs with the clean mountain air, then started off in search of Pippa.

Busy, scheduled-to-the-hilt Pippa could be anywhere, he mused, doing just about anything. She was, whether she realized it or not, adept at a great many things. He'd bet she could handle the reservations at one of the hotel-casinos in Vegas with no problem. While Miracles was only a gaming casino, the majority of the other big places were also hotels. Jared could pull some strings and get her a job.

Nick shook his head. No, he knew she would never go for that. She'd insist on doing it all on her own. He'd know after the fact about her new job in Vegas and where she had chosen to live. Oh, yes, he was really hating this.

He didn't even bother to stop at her cabin, knowing she had been up and out hours before. He went, instead, to the store and found Grandma and Grandpa Pauling behind the counter.

"Good morning," he said. "Well, I guess it's nearly noon." Grandma had a gleam in her eye, he noted. It was as though she could peer into his brain and discover that he and Pippa were lovers. Grandma didn't seem upset by the knowledge, but it was a tad disconcerting to be so aware that she knew. "Do you know where Pippa is?"

"She's gone for a walk with Emma," Grandma said. "Pippa is telling her about the move to Las Vegas."

"Oh, I see. Well, I guess I'll wait until they show up. I wouldn't want to interrupt them." He paused. "Pippa told me about her childhood. I've asked her to marry me, but she won't until she's proven to herself that she can provide a home for herself and Emma. I don't like it but there's not much I can do about it."

"Have patience, Nick," Grandma said.

"That's what I keep telling myself. Have you folks decided where you'd like to live?"

"There's a retirement community down in Phoenix we've had our eye on," Grandma said. "They have all kinds of activities, and different-size homes to choose from."

"Sounds good. It isn't that far from Phoenix to Las Vegas, either. I know you'll want to see Pippa and Emma as often as possible. Did you talk to the realtor?"

"Yes," Grandpa said. "She called back a while ago. She's coming up from Phoenix tomorrow with an offer from the developer who's been wanting this land for years. This could all happen very quickly."

"It'll be best if it does," Grandma said. "No sense moping around about things. The sooner we get on with it, the better."

"Amen to that," Nick said. "I'd like to marry Pippa right here at Serenity Cove."

"Patience, Nick," Grandma said, laughing. "Patience."

"Yeah." He shoved his hands into his pockets, and began to wander around the store on the outside chance that he might have missed seeing something.

Pippa sat with Emma under a tree near the lake. The grass was dry and warm from the sun, despite the heavy rain of the day before.

"Do they have first grade there?" Emma asked.

"Oh, yes," Pippa said. "You'll make lots of new friends in Las Vegas. I know you'll miss Grandma and Grandpa, but they'll visit us often."

"That's good," Emma said. "Nick will be there, so we have one friend already."

Pippa smiled. "Yes, Nick will be there."

"Will we have to live on top of a mountain again, Mommy?"

Pippa studied her daughter. "No, we won't live on top of a mountain, but I thought you liked it here at Serenity Cove, Emma."

"It's okay, but I don't have anyone to play with. My friends down in town get to play together all the time. I want to live in a town 'stead of on a mountain."

"Oh, Emma, I had no idea you were lonely living up here," Pippa said, feeling her throat tighten. "Why didn't you tell me?"

" 'Cause this is where *you* live. I always want to live where you live, Mommy."

Pippa wrapped her arms tightly around her daughter. "Oh, sweetheart, I thought this was the best place for us. I can see now that it was best for me, but not for you. We're going to be fine in Las Vegas, both of us, and you'll have oodles of friends."

"How come they call it Lost Vegas? Do people get lost there?"

"No, no." Only those who get caught up and lost in the gambling fever, she thought. "It's Las Vegas, not Lost Vegas."

"Oh. And Grandma and Grandpa are going to live in Phoenix but come see us?"

"Absolutely."

"Can I still have my birthday party?"

"Oh, yes, of course. It will be awhile before we move."

"I want to go right after my birthday, Mommy. Then I'll be ready for first grade and all my new friends. Can we go then? Can we?"

"I don't know for sure, Emma, but I'll tell you as soon as I do."

"Okay. Can I go tell Grandma and Grandpa that I'm going to have new friends? I bet they're happy, 'cause they can have friends, too, 'stead of living on top of a mountain. Can I go?"

"Yes, I'll see you later at the store. I love you, Emma."

"I love you, too, Mommy." She jumped to her feet and ran up the slope.

Pippa watched Emma until the little girl had disappeared from view, then drew her legs up and wrapped her arms around them.

"Oh, Emma, I didn't know you were lonely here," she

whispered. She rested her forehead on her knees and fought threatening tears.

Emma had been lonely, she thought. Dear Lord, why hadn't she seen it? Why hadn't she recognized in her own child what she had felt herself as a little girl? She'd been so sure she'd given Emma all that had been lacking in her own life after her father had died, but she'd been wrong, so very wrong.

"Pippa?"

She looked up to see Nick standing beside her. "Hello."

"You're upset. Didn't it go well with Emma?"

"She's very excited about moving to Las Vegas."

"May I sit down?"

"Yes, of course."

He lowered himself to the ground and rested his back against the tree. "Then why are there tears in your eyes?"

"Oh, Nick, Emma has been lonely living up here. She was afraid we'd have to go to the top of another mountain. I didn't know, didn't see what was happening to my own child. All I was thinking about was myself and my own needs."

"Hey, you're being too rough on yourself. Emma is basically happy at Serenity Cove. I can see where living in a city would hold great appeal for her, though."

"She wants to go right after her birthday party."

"Sounds good to me," Nick said, smiling at her. He wrapped his arm around her shoulders and tugged gently until she released her hold on her knees and moved closer to him. "Don't beat yourself up over what Emma said. This was a great place to raise a baby. Now that Emma is ready for school, she'll be in a city that offers her a lot of opportunities. It's all working out fine. The realtor is coming up tomorrow with an offer for Serenity Cove."

Pippa's eyes widened. "So soon?"

"Yep. Grandma and Grandpa are pleased as punch. I think Grandpa already sees himself golfing at that retirement community in Phoenix."

"Emma said she bet they would be glad to leave this mountain too."

"I'd say they're ready."

"Do you realize that if Serenity Cove had continued to prosper, I would have kept Emma here all through her growing-up years? I wouldn't have met her needs, made her happy, any more than my mother did for me. I can't believe this. I've been so selfish."

"Pippa, stop it," Nick said firmly. "You did the best thing possible when you brought Emma here. It's time for change, that's all, and you're making those changes."

"Only because I was forced to. I would have just stayed on here, not seeing how lonely Emma was."

"Oh, I don't know about that. I'm in this picture, remember? I would have asked you to leave here with me even if Serenity Cove were making a million bucks a year. You and Emma were destined to live in Las Vegas, my love. It was written in the stars, or the moon, or whatever."

She smiled. "You always have an answer for everything."

"No, Pippa, I don't," he said seriously. "I'd like the answer to how to convince you to marry me right now, but I can't find that one."

"Nick . . ."

"Yeah, I know." He raised one hand to silence her. "I'd rather not go through it from the top again. Look, let's drive down to that dinky little town. I want to get Emma a birthday present."

"Oh, I can't. I have things I have to do."

"Pippa, please, chuck your schedule this once, will you? We'll drive down, have some lunch, shop, and be back in a couple of hours. Just nod and smile to agree."

She laughed. "I can't speak?"

"Nope. Just nod."

"I can't say, 'I love you, Nick Capoletti'? I can't say that you are the dearest, sweetest, most magnificent man I've ever known? I can't say—"

Whatever Pippa might have said next was silenced by Nick's mouth coming down hard on hers. He slipped his tongue between her lips and she met it eagerly with her own. The kiss was heated, hungry, and all too soon it was over.

"This, ma'am," Nick said, his voice rough, "is not the time or the place. You're going to have to stop kissing me right now, like it or not."

"What a shame."

"True. Ready to go to town?"

She nodded.

"Now you're getting the hang of it, kid." He got to his feet and extended his hand to her. "What's the name of this bustling burg we're going to?"

She took his hand and allowed him to pull her up next to him. Heat throbbed low in her body from the passionate kiss, and her gaze fell on his compelling mouth.

"Don't look at me like that," he said. "Just tell me the name of the town."

She blinked. "Oh. Sorry. It's called Gold Dust."

He hooted with laughter. "Gold Dust, Arizona? That, Miss Pippa, is corny."

She shrugged. "It's quaint, befitting the area." They started up the grassy slope, Pippa's hand still tucked in Nick's. "It's better than Lost Vegas. Emma thought that was what I'd said."

He chuckled. "Vegas isn't lost. A million tourists a year know exactly where it is."

"I straightened Emma out on that, though I couldn't help but think that there are lost souls there, those who get the gambling fever. Lives can be destroyed by that disease. That type of entertainment has never held any appeal for me. I think I'll pretend that part of the city just isn't there. It's so . . . false. I've seen pictures of the casinos, and they seem . . . I don't know . . . from another world. Each one is flashier than the next, all trying to entice people to come inside and lose their hard-earned money. When I contact a rental agency to help me find a place to live, I'll tell them I want to be as far away from that section of the city as possible." She paused. "I need to stop by my cabin to get my purse, then tell Grandma we're going to town."

"Yeah, fine." Nick said absently. Oh, brother, he was in trouble. He'd started to tell Pippa on several occasions that he worked at Miracles Casino, but the timing had never seemed right. They'd been covering so much territory so fast, they hadn't yet gotten to what he did for a living. She was going to pretend that the casinos didn't exist? He lived in one! He had good friends at Miracles, a sense of family, and he earned excellent money as Jared's second-in-command. Dammit, just what he needed. Another stumbling block in the way to getting Pippa to agree to marry him. "The casinos bring important revenues into the city," he said lamely. Lord, what a dumb thing to say.

"Money people have worked very hard for. I'm just

not comfortable with the whole concept." They stopped in front of her cabin. "Do you want to come in?"

"No. I'll go get my car and pick you up at the store."

"Okay." She brushed her lips over his, then hurried into the cabin.

Nick started off down the path. "I didn't need this," he muttered. "This is going to be a beaut of a hassle; I can feel it in my bones. Oh, dammit."

In her cabin Pippa strode across the living room to get her purse from the desk. As she snatched it up, her glance fell on the rather worn registration card Nick had filled out and Grandpa had delivered. She picked it up and scanned it quickly.

It was a joke, she thought frantically, feeling the color drain from her face. Nick had listed his address as Miracles Casino, Las Vegas, Nevada, and the person to notify in case of emergency as Jared Loring at the same address. For his occupation Nick had written, "Administrative Assistant, Miracles Casino." Yes, yes, it was a joke. Dear, wonderful, gentle Nick didn't work in a casino. And heaven knew he certainly didn't live in one. That was crazy. He wouldn't fit into that fake lifestyle where the only thing that mattered was winning money. Not Nick.

She shook her head and pulled a new registration card from a slot in the desk. Mr. Capoletti had had his fun, she decided, but during lunch he could fill out a fresh card—properly this time. Even though Serenity Cove would soon be a thing of the past, Pippa Pauling kept accurate records.

Besides, she reasoned, she was definitely due to know just what the man she loved did for a living. His clothes and car said that his job paid well, whatever it was. Did he own a house? Live in an apartment? Well, they'd chat about it over lunch. But one thing was for certain: Nick Capoletti didn't live and work in a casino!

Nick's car was a bronze-colored sedan that hugged the twisting, turning mountain roads. He'd gone through the flashy-sports-car stage while in college, he told Pippa as they drove down the mountain.

This was how it should be, she thought during a lull in their conversation about movies and books. Two people in love talking, sharing anything and everything. She'd never known a relationship like this, where she could just be herself and feel so important, as though everything she said was interesting and special. Love was glorious, and she'd chosen well after waiting so many years for it. Nick Capoletti was everything, and even more than, she might have fantasized about in the quiet hours of the night.

"This is it," she said as they at last reached the desert floor. "Gold Dust, Arizona. The entire two blocks of it. The kids from around here are bused to school in Timberville, which is a bigger town another fifteen miles down. Timberville has a lumber mill, a lot of artists, retired people, and workers from the pecan orchards."

Nick laughed. "Thank you, Madam Chamber of Commerce. You did that very well."

"Thank you, sir," she said, smiling. "Please note the small, very small, department store coming up on your right. Beyond that is a small, very small, café where we can have lunch."

"I had a late breakfast, but you must be hungry. Do you want to eat before we shop for Emma's present?"

"No, we can shop first." She laughed. "My level of hunger at the moment is small, very small."

Nick parked the car, then turned in his seat to look at her. He reached out one hand to weave his fingers through her dark hair.

"It's so good to see you like this," he said. "You're relaxed, happy, and your laughter is like beautiful music."

She turned her head to kiss the palm of his hand. "It feels wonderful to laugh, Nick. It feels wonderful to be with you like this. You're right, you know, about my rigid schedules and routines. It's time that I learned to bend the rules, be open to ideas that will bring more laughter to my life and Emma's. I still believe she needs the security of a set pattern in her life, but I definitely overdid it. There should be room for picnics and popcorn and outings like this one."

"I love you," Nick said, his voice slightly husky. "What you just said was very special, and I'll treasure it. Not only because it will make a difference, a nice difference, in your and Emma's lives, but because it means you really listened to what I said, believed in me enough to weigh and measure my words. Oh, Pippa, we're going to be so good together, have such a fantastic life. It will be give and take, back and forth, a blending of our ideas, hopes, dreams."

"I guess . . . Well, I guess that's what love is all about," she said softly.

"I guess you're right. It's part of the magic."

Neither moved, as their gazes stayed locked in loving warmth. It was a special moment, which marked the gaining of greater understanding, commitment, and love between them. Then slowly the messages of desire become clear, and an even greater awareness seemed to hum in the air.

Nick cleared his throat. "I think we'd better get out of this car before we shock the citizens of Gold Dust, Arizona, when I do what I want to and your eyes are telling me you want me to do."

Pippa blinked, as if bringing the car and the town back into focus. "Oh. Yes, of course. What do you think you want to get Emma?"

"Finger paints."

She groaned. "No. Take pity on me. Finger paints are a mother's nightmare." She opened the car door. "Goodness, I'm glad you didn't come down here alone."

Nick got out of the car. That was the bottom line, he mused. He didn't want to be alone in life, not anymore, not since finding Pippa. He didn't want to wait while she struck out on her own in Vegas, either. What they had was so damn good. If only she'd agree to marry him now, so they could really start their life together. If only . . .

"Coming?" she asked, from the sidewalk.

"Yeah, sure." He closed the car door and joined her, immediately circling her shoulders with his arm and tucking her next to him. He inhaled her fresh, feminine aroma, felt her soft curves nestled to his hard body, and dropped a kiss on the top of her head. "No finger paints, huh?"

"No!"

In the limited toy section of the very small store Nick examined everything. He finally decided on a giant box of crayons and a thick coloring book.

"Very good," Pippa said, nodding her approval. "Emma will love her gift."

"There's nothing better than a new box of crayons. They even smell good. I wonder if she'll let me color with her if I promise not to use the red first."

Oh, how she loved this man, Pippa though happily as she followed Nick to the counter.

The café was classic, Nick declared. It had red vinyl on the booths and menus enclosed in cracked plastic folders. They ordered stew and cornbread and tall glasses of milk. The food was delicious, and Nick asked for apple pie with ice cream for dessert. Pippa declined dessert, saying she was stuffed. As Nick attacked his pie, she watched him with love shining in her eyes.

"Oh," she said, opening her purse, "I almost forgot." She pulled out the registration card and a pen and set them in front of him. "There. Even though Serenity Cove is about to go out of business, let it never be said that Pippa Pauling didn't keep accurate records."

He frowned at the card. "I filled out one of those already."

"Very funny, Mr. Capoletti," she said, smiling at him. "I finally got around to looking at it."

"Funny?"

"Putting down your address as 'Miracles Casino.' You're not exactly the type of man who would actually work and live in one of those places." She laughed. "It would be a terrible influence on Peaches. So start over on that card. Besides, it's time I knew what you do for a living, don't you think?"

Oh, boy, Nick thought glumly, this was it. He really would have preferred not to have this discussion in a greasy spoon but it didn't appear he was going to have any choice in the matter. He wasn't the "type of man" who would work in a casino? What "type" of people did she think ran the casinos and hotels? Adding that remark to what she'd said earlier about not wanting to live anywhere near the gambling section of Vegas, he knew this was not going to go well. His stew and pie were now a painful brick in his stomach, and he would have liked to postpone the entire conversation.

"Sir?" Pippa said, still smiling. "Would you be so kind as to fill out a new card? Correctly, this time?"

"Pippa," he said in a low voice, "the card I filled out before had the information on it that you want. The *correct* information."

"Don't be silly. You don't live and work . . ." Her smile faded. "Nick?"

He took her hands in his and looked directly into her wide eyes.

"Listen to me," he said. "You have preconceived ideas about the casinos, about the type, as you put it, of people who own them and work in them. That's not fair, Pippa. They're businesses like any other, making a profit, providing jobs for a great many people. It takes a lot of hard work and long hours to keep a casino running in the black. I'm proud of what I do, and I'm very fond of the people at Miracles I have the privilege—privilege, Pippa—of working with. They're good, decent human beings who are more family than friends. They're there if you need them, no matter what, no questions asked. They'll welcome you and Emma with open arms."

"No," she said, shaking her head. "I won't allow Emma anywhere near your precious Miracles." She pulled her hands free and pressed one to her forehead. "I can't believe this. I thought it was a joke. You even live there? Oh, dear heaven."

"We'll get a house once we're married. I know we can't raise Emma at Miracles. I'll talk to Jared, too, about having some of my duties changed so I don't have to work the night shift all the time." He frowned. "Dammit, would you quit looking at me as if I'd just grown an extra nose? I make excellent money doing an honest day's work. I can provide very well for you and Emma. There is nothing tainted or sordid about being a part of Miracles. You'll come to realize that once you get to know the people. I have important responsibilities there, and I'm good at my job."

"A job that pays you from money lost by other people. You lure them in with false promises—even the name suggests that wonderful things are going to happen inside that place, but they lose. Lives are destroyed by gambling fever, Nick. How can you live with that knowledge?"

His jaw tightened. "You've got a totally distorted picture of it all. It's only a few who can't stop once they start. The rest are on vacation, having a wonderful time, spending only what they decided beforehand they could afford. We provide a service, a brief escape from reality, from the pressures and stress of everyday life. That's what vacations are all about. The casinos are like an adult Disneyland, a place to go for a while for just plain old fun. Your concept is wrong, and I can prove it to you."

"But it's not real. It's all phony glamour. Nick, what do you wear when you're on duty at the casino?"

He slouched back in the booth. "Come on, Pippa."

"Tell me. What do you wear?"

"A tuxedo. A very expensive custom-tailored tuxedo." His voice started to rise. "Every inch of Miracles is first class. It's a glamorous, opulent place that makes everyone who walks through the doors feel important, deserving of the finest. Our attire emphasizes that. We put on our best because we're welcoming special guests."

"And their money," she said tightly.

Nick glanced around and saw that their heated conversation was drawing the undivided attention of the half-dozen other people in the café. He slid out of the booth and dropped ten dollars onto the table.

"Let's get out of here," he said gruffly. "I don't feel like being the entertainment in this place."

Her back ramrod-straight, she followed him out of the café. Her mind was whirling from the impact of Nick's words.

He lived and worked in a casino. That wasn't what an ordinary family man, a husband and father, did. Nick was part of a world she didn't approve of. She couldn't understand what drew people in droves to squander their money and bask in what wasn't real. And she couldn't understand how Nick could possibly wish to be a part of all that. The whole concept was foreign and frightening.

They drove out of Gold Dust in silence, the tension in the car seeming to crackle through the air. When Pippa slid a glance at Nick, she saw his tight grip on the steering wheel, the hard line to his jaw.

"Pippa," he said finally, "you're standing in judgment of something you know nothing about. I realize that your mother became part of a lifestyle you couldn't comprehend, and you suffered because of it. Now, I guess, you think it's happening again, but you're wrong. There is nothing off the wall about my career choice. I have administrative duties that could be adapted to any large business. I'm at Miracles because I sincerely like what I do and the people I work with. You'd like those people, too, if you'd give them a chance."

"I never dreamed . . . When I saw your card I thought it was a joke, I really did. I'm stunned by this, and I don't seem to be able to get a handle on it."

"Because you still have images in your mind of how it was when your father was alive. I'm not a banker, my hours aren't the same day after day, but I can work out a decent schedule with Jared. Still, Pippa, you've got to give a little, compromise. And Lord knows you've got to lighten up your attitude. I don't stand by the door of Miracles pointing a gun at people and forcing them to hand over their life's savings. They've chosen to come to Las Vegas. They want exactly what we're offering. There is nothing wrong with what I do for a living! You tried to mold Bill Pauling into a clone of your father, and look what that got you. Well, listen up, lady. You're not going to have any luck trying to rework me, either. You'd better get that straight right now."

That stank, Capoletti, Nick raged at himself. He was pushing Pippa to the wall, and dragging up her past in the bargain. It was because of her past that she was scared to death of anything out of the ordinary, anything she didn't fully understand. He'd lost his temper and slam-dunked her with words he never should have spoken. Dammit, he was blowing this so badly, he should be shot.

"I'm sorry," he said quietly. "I shouldn't have said that."

She stared down at her hands, clenched tightly in her lap. "You're right. I did try to change Bill into what I needed him to be. So he left me, because that wasn't who he wanted to be."

"I'm not going to leave you, Pippa, but I'm not going to quit my job because it upsets you. I'm asking you to meet me halfway on this, give Miracles and the people there a chance. My half will be to arrange better hours so we can function as a family. I'll still have to work some nights, but not all of the time." He glanced over at her, then quickly redirected his attention to the winding mountain road. "Pippa, please, give it and me a chance."

She nodded. "That's only fair, isn't it? I'll—I'll move to Las Vegas as planned, find a place to live and a job, and I'll have plenty of time to see what Miracles is all about, won't I? I realize I sound very prejudiced, and I hate prejudice in any form. So! I'll give myself a stern lecture about having an open mind about your career." She nodded again. "Yes, I'll do that."

She was falling apart, Nick thought. Her voice was quivering, and she was going to break her fingers off if she gripped them any more tightly. She'd have her own place to live and plenty of time? Hell, it was going to take a stick of dynamite to pry her out of her own safe little place if she didn't come around. He was fighting the shadows of her past, and he was doing a lousy job of it.

Serenity Cove came into view, and he cringed when he heard Pippa's sigh of relief.

"Where should I drop you off?" he asked, knowing he sounded weary.

"The store. I want to get Emma. She can tag along with me while I weed the flower beds. She's my responsibility, not the Paulings'. I'd better get used to that, since I'll be alone in Vegas."

Nick felt the brick in his stomach grow to the size of a bowling ball. He pulled up in front of the store, but didn't turn off the ignition.

"I'll see you later, Pippa."

"Yes. Fine." She slid out of the car and closed the door without looking at him.

Nick smacked the steering wheel with the heel of his hand and cut loose with a string of Italian expletives as he drove away. He was definitely losing his touch at being charming.

Inside the store, Pippa asked Grandpa where Emma was.

"Oh, she and Grandma went down by the lake to pick wildflowers. Did you have a nice time in town with Nick?"

"Not really," Pippa said, staring at the jar of jaw-breakers. "It started out really fun, but . . . Grandpa, Nick lives and works in a casino in Las Vegas." She slowly shifted her gaze to look at him.

"I know. I read his card after he gave it to me. I'm going to try my luck on some nickel slot machines at Miracles when we come to visit you. Always wanted to fiddle with one of those gizmos."

Pippa's eyes widened. "You wouldn't. Would you? You'd put your hard-earned money into one of those machines and watch it be gobbled up?"

"Well, mercy's sake, Pippa, I'm not planning on pouring a bundle into the thing. I figure I'll get me a jar and toss my nickels into it when I have loose change. That will be my fund. Yep, I'm looking forward to that. Grandma said it sounded like fun, when I told her, but I said she'd have to get her own jar to save up her nickels."

"You're *both* going to gamble?" Pippa asked. "And just how do you expect me to explain that to Emma? I can't fathom how I'll tell her what Nick does for a living, let alone that her grandparents have gambling jars filling up with nickels."

"What are you all in a dither about? Is that what spoiled your trip to town with Nick, learning what his job is?"

"I was shocked, Grandpa." She folded her arms around her waist. "I've seen pictures of those casinos, seen the gaudy way they're decorated, the flashy clothes the people who work there wear. Did you know that Nick wears a custom-tailored tuxedo to work? A tuxedo, for heaven's sake. That's not a normal father image for Emma. He doesn't work regular hours, either. He said he'll change his schedule, but he'd still have to work some nights. Work? Taking people's money, that's what it is, including your nickels, Grandpa. Nick says Miracles provides a service that people want. I think it's disgusting, and I never dreamed he was a part of that. I told him I'd give it all a chance, be fair and open-minded, but how can I do that?"

"By getting off your soapbox, Miss High and Mighty," Grandpa said sternly. "Have you ever been inside one of those casinos? No. Yet there you stand, deciding Nick's career doesn't measure up to your standards. Did it ever occur to you that he could have felt your helping to run this poor, dilapidated place doesn't measure up to *his* standards? But he didn't do that, did he? He fell in love with you, not Serenity Cove. You're punishing Nick for things done to you in the past, Pippa. Things he had nothing to do with. You're darn tootin' you'd better give Miracles a fair chance, young lady, or you stand to lose that man. And from where I'm sitting, he's the best thing ever to happen to you, and to Emma. You've got some serious thinking to do, and I'd suggest you get started."

"Well!" Pippa said, planting her hands on her hips. "Thank you for the sermon."

"You're welcome," Grandpa said pleasantly. "It needed to be said, and I said it. I feel better for it, too."

"Bully for you."

She yanked the lid off the jar of jawbreakers, grabbed a big blue one, and shoved it into her mouth. Then, looking like a lopsided chipmunk, with the candy jammed into one cheek, she stomped toward the door.

"Think while you're pouting," Grandpa called after her.

Pippa was unable to deliver a snappy retort, thanks to the hard lump of candy in her mouth, so made her point by slamming the door instead.

"I hope you don't lose Nick Capoletti, Pippa," Grandpa said to no one. "Oh, honey, I sure hope you don't."

Seven

Nick spent a long, restless evening alone, and an even longer night tossing and turning in bed. The scattered dreams he had were about Pippa, who always remained just out of his reach.

After showering and dressing, he sat at the kitchen table and sipped hot coffee. He was in such a gloomy mood he didn't even feel like talking to Peaches. His plan had been to leave Pippa alone to sort through their conversation about Miracles, in the hope that she would realize she had unfairly judged a situation she knew nothing about.

It had been a lousy plan, he now deduced. Pippa hadn't come within ten feet of him since he'd left her off at the store, and that did not speak well of his current status with her. He didn't have time to waste, as his week at Serenity Cove was flying by, and he would have to leave early on his final day to make the long, hot desert drive back to Vegas.

"So, Peaches," he said, "I need a new plan. It would help if I knew what it was."

He left his cabin and strolled toward the store, practicing various greetings in his mind that he might use when he saw Pippa. He ran the gamut from bright and breezy to macho and surly.

In all honesty, he admitted, he was shooting in the dark. He had no idea what he was doing. Being in love was enormously confusing. It was proving to be no easy task to blend two lives into one. Love did not, unfortunately, conquer all. It was no wonder people made a fortune writing books on how to have a smooth-sailing relationship with a member of the opposite sex. These were rough seas to be sailing on.

He was compromising, doing his part. He was stepping back and waiting for Pippa to prove to herself that she was capable of supporting herself and Emma. He was willing to speak to Jared about juggling his duties and hours. He'd agreed to take over the night shift at Miracles after Jared married Tabor, but Jared would surely see that Nick, too, wanted the majority of his evenings free. There were others trained to supervise the gaming floor, and Nick and Jared could take turns being on call for emergencies. Nick's paperwork, his overseeing of the pickup and delivery of money, the hiring of employees, and all his other duties could be tended to during the day.

So, his job at Miracles should present no problem if, and it was a big *if*, Pippa was willing to view his work with an open mind. What was she thinking this morning? She had compromised, too, by agreeing to test her wings in Vegas, where he would be close by. Would she go the next step—push aside her preconceived notions of casinos and those who worked in them and give Miracles a fair chance? She had to. They couldn't be tripped up now, lose all they'd found together. No way. He wasn't going to give up the only woman he'd ever loved.

As he approached the store, he saw Emma sitting on the front steps, playing with Ben the doll. He quickened his pace to cover the remaining distance.

"Hello, Emma," he said, stopping in front of her. "How's Ben?"

"Fine. I get to take Ben with me when we move to Las Vegas. I get to take all my toys, and my clothes too."

"You bet, sugar. Ben will like Vegas, and so will you." He glanced up and saw the "Closed" sign on the store door. "Is something wrong with the store?"

"No. Mommy, Grandma, and Grandpa are having a 'portant meeting with a lady 'bout selling Serenity Cove. Mommy said since I was nearly six I could stay out here by myself. I can't go by the lake or anything 'cause Mommy needs to know where I am."

Nick lowered himself to the step. "I'll keep you company, okay?"

"Sure. Mommy likes to know where you are too. She talks 'bout you a lot."

"Oh, yeah?" Was it rotten to wiggle information out of a little kid? Nick wondered. Well, tough. Desperate men did desperate things. "What does she say about me?"

Emma shrugged. "Stuff."

Wonderful. "Like what?"

"Oh, you know, that you're really nice, and you gots a plant named Peaches. Mommy smiled real pretty when she told me about Peaches. She said she was happy that you came here."

Oh, hey, this was getting good, Nick thought. His gloomy mood was definitely improving. "Well, I'm happy that I came here too," he said. "I like you and your mom a lot, Emma."

She stopped fiddling with Ben's dress and looked directly at Nick. "I like you bunches, Nick, I really do, and if you like me and Mommy, then maybe you could be our daddy. Think so?"

Uh-oh, Nick thought, searching his mind for an answer. He couldn't say that his status as daddy would be a *fait accompli* if Emma's mommy didn't have such a stubborn streak. Pippa would have strangled him with her bare hands. Think, Capoletti. Say something brilliant.

"Well, I . . . um . . . Well, that's certainly an interesting thought, Emma." Oh, for crying out loud.

She leaned toward him. "Do you want to be our daddy? Do you want to have a baby brother?"

He laughed. "The CIA needs you, Emma."

"Huh?"

"Look, sweetheart, that's something I have to decide with your mom. But I'll tell you this. If I were going to have a little girl, I'd pick you. It makes me very proud to know that you'd like me to be your daddy. I don't know yet what's going to happen, so we'll have to wait and be surprised." What a bunch of bull. He couldn't lose Pippa and Emma! "Okay?"

"No," Emma said, wrinkling her nose. "Why can't you and Mommy decide today?"

"Out of the mouths of babes," he muttered.

"What?"

"So, are you all set for your birthday party?" he asked, smiling brightly. "Birthdays are great, aren't they? Yes, sir, there's nothing finer than a birthday."

He breathed a sigh of relief as Emma launched into a lengthy dissertation about the plans for the long-awaited birthday party. He nodded and smiled in what he hoped were the appropriate places, but he was actually thinking about Pippa.

So she had been talking about him to Emma, he mused. Emma was definitely in his court. He knew some guys who had been put through the wringer because their ladies' children couldn't stand them. All systems were go with Miss Emma. It was Mother Pippa who was holding up the show. Patience, Capoletti, patience.

The door to the store opened, and Grandpa came out with an attractive woman in her forties. Nick stood and moved up onto the porch to get out of the way.

"Morning, Nick," Grandpa said. "You and Emma can go on in now, if you'd like. We've wrapped up our business. Mrs. Nelson, this is Nick Capoletti."

"How do you do?" Mrs. Nelson said, extending her hand to Nick.

He shook her hand. "Fine. Nice to meet you."

"I'll see Mrs. Nelson to her car," Grandpa said, "then talk to you inside, Nick."

He nodded, feeling like a boy being sent to the principal's office. At least Pippa was in there. Maybe there was safety in numbers.

"Come on, Emma," he said.

He saw Pippa the moment he stepped inside. She was standing by the counter with Grandma, wearing a pink blouse and a pink flowered wraparound skirt. Her hair was a dark, shiny tumble down her back. She looked, he decided, good enough to eat.

Emma ran in ahead of him, and Pippa smiled at the little girl, then slowly met Nick's gaze. Her smile faded as she walked toward him. When she was so close, he could have drunk in the aroma of her floral cologne, she stopped, looking directly into his eyes. His heart thundered in his chest.

"Nick, I'm sorry," she said quietly. "I didn't behave

well yesterday. I don't seem to be able to handle anything new or different, anything I don't fully understand, and that's very childish. But that's the problem, isn't it? I haven't had much practice at being grown up."

"That's not true."

"Yes, it is, but I'm working on that. If you still want me to, I'll move to Vegas. I'll consider Miracles with an open mind, or at least try my best to. I really am sorry, and I really do love you."

"Oh, Pippa." He pulled her close, wrapping his arms tightly around her, "I love you so much," he whispered.

"Grandma, Grandma," Emma said, hopping up and down, "Nick is hugging my mommy. I betcha they're deciding to be a mommy and daddy for me."

"Oh, dear," Pippa said, wiggling out of Nick's embrace.

He chuckled, then looked up as Grandpa came back into the store.

"Grandpa," Emma said, "Nick hugged my mommy and—"

"Emma," Pippa interrupted, "that's enough. Big people hug each other all the time, and it doesn't mean . . . That is . . ."

"Yes?" Nick said, all innocence. "You were saying?"

Grandpa laughed, then walked across the store to Grandma.

"Well, it's done," he said, still smiling. "We signed the papers accepting the offer the developer made. He's buying everything as it is—the cabins, furniture, store stock, the works. He owns other places where the furniture can be used, and he'll pull the cabins down before the first snow. Pippa will write and cancel all the reservations for after this weekend. Mrs. Nelson will put through the closing papers in what they call an 'express transaction,' because the developer is paying cash. We have two weeks to pack up and go."

"Whew," Nick said. "Nobody's wasting any time."

"No need to," Grandma said. "The title is clear on this land, the man is paying cash, that's it."

"You own all this free and clear?" Nick asked.

"Yep," Grandpa said. "Have for many years. We'll have a hefty nest egg, and so will Pippa."

"Me?" she said. "No, not me. I've been living here rent free all these years. None of that money is mine. You paid me a salary besides giving us a home."

"We paid you what you agreed to take," Grandma said, "which wasn't nearly enough, considering all the work you did. So we've been keeping track of the rest in a ledger. It's all there for you to see, Pippa. That money is yours, and you'll have it when the deal goes through. It will give you enough for a fine start in Las Vegas and you'll have an emergency fund besides. Don't bother to argue, because that's how it's going to be."

"But—" she started to say.

"Don't bother to argue," Nick said, laughing. "These people obviously can be as stubborn as you."

"Darn tootin'," Grandpa said. "Pippa, I'm going down to town to get some boxes to start packing. Is it all right if Emma comes along?"

"What?" Pippa asked, appearing rather dazed. "Oh, yes, of course."

Emma skipped across the room. "You can hug my mommy again while I'm gone, Nick."

"Thank you," he said seriously. "I'll certainly do that."

"Shoo," Grandma said, flapping her hands at them. "I have things to do."

"Yes, ma'am." Nick grabbed Pippa's hand and pulled her out the door behind Grandpa and Emma. "Come on, space case. Let's go for a walk."

They were halfway to the lake before she spoke. "I can't take that money."

"Yes, you can, Pippa. The Paulings know how hard you work here. You've been seeing your life here from an emotional standpoint. They included a practical business angle as well. This is how they want to do it, so let them. They know you well enough to understand you wouldn't accept the money as a gift, so they're prepared to show you on paper that you've earned it. *Earned* it, Pippa. If you could get it through your head that you've been supporting yourself and Emma ever since you got here, we could—Never mind. I've agreed to our deal and I'll keep my mouth shut."

The lake came into view, and he steered her toward a big tree.

"You look sensational today," he said. "Can you sit on the ground in that pretty skirt?"

She nodded, and they settled on the grass beneath the tree, their backs against the trunk.

"You seem like you're in a daze," he said.

She pressed her hands to her cheeks. "So much is happening so quickly, my head is spinning, Nick. I'm frightened, but I'm excited at the same time. My whole life is being turned upside down."

"And your heart?" he asked, drawing one thumb gently over her soft cheek. "How's your heart doing?"

She smiled. "I love you. My heart is doing fine."

He brushed his lips across hers. "Good." He paused. "I guess I'm going to repeat this spiel after all. I just have to, because it's so damn important."

"What are you talking about?"

"Pippa, please, somewhere in the middle of that muddle in your brain, grab hold of the fact that you've earned your keep here. Everyone is aware of that except you. You aren't a child who mooched off your relatives all these years. You worked hard, provided a home for Emma, performed valuable and varied tasks in the running of Serenity Cove. No, don't say anything, just think about it when things calm down a bit. You're determined to prove to yourself something you've already accomplished. None of us can convince you of that, I guess. You'll have to figure it out for yourself. Just promise me you'll think about it."

"Yes, all right. I'll think about it."

"You're probably saying that just to humor me, but I'll take what I can get." He kissed her quickly again. "Lord, I missed you last night. All of yesterday after I dropped you at the store was hell. I figured you needed some time alone, but I was miserable. I didn't even feel like talking to Peaches. Have you noticed that love can be a very debilitating emotion?"

She laughed. "I've noticed."

"I like it, though. No, I love it. I love being in love. How's that?"

"Don't you ever get frightened by it all?"

"Only when I think that I might lose you. I was really shaking when you reacted the way you did about my job, but you'll see it's nothing to be upset over. You're giving it a chance, and that's all I can ask. There's only one thing standing in our way now, Pippa, and that's you. This need to prove yourself . . . Well, I've said enough on the subject. You've promised to think about all you've done here, and I intend to hold you to that promise."

She nodded.

"Emma gave me permission to hug you," he added. "Do you suppose I could sneak a kiss or two into the deal?"

"I'm sure you can, Mr. Capoletti. A kiss or two, or three, or—"

He captured her mouth with his in a searing kiss that went on and on. Pippa leaned against him, seeking more, wanting more, aching for more. Nick slowly, reluctantly lifted his head.

"You have reservations to cancel," he said, his voice rough.

She sighed. "Yes. I'd better go. Would you like to have dinner with Emma and me tonight?"

"Yes, I'd like that very much."

"Six o'clock."

"Fine. I wish I were going to be here for Emma's birthday party. Next year I'll be on the scene. Lord knows she'll need all the support she can get when her teeth start to fall out. That is major-trauma time."

Pippa gazed at the lake. "Next year," she said, rather wistfully. "Do you ever wish you had a crystal ball that would give you a glimpse of the future?"

He took one of her hands with his, resting them on his thigh. "No. Pippa, I fell in love with you a heartbeat or two after I saw you. I wasn't prepared for it, didn't know it was going to happen, but there it was. I will never forget, or take for granted, the way I felt, the incredible warmth and joy that filled me to overflowing. If I'd had a crystal ball, I would have known what to expect when I arrived here. I would have said, 'Oh, yeah, that's right, this is where I find the woman I'm going to fall in love with.' No, no crystal ball. These emotions are too special, too honest and real, to allow anything to take the edge off of them."

"That was beautiful," she said.

He shrugged. "That's how I feel."

"I'll cancel the order for the crystal ball."

"Oh, okay," he said, chuckling.

"Oh, Nick, I'm going to miss Serenity Cove. Emma and I have had a good life here. She took her first steps here, said her first words . . . so many memories. I'll miss Grandma and Grandpa, too. Goodness, I'd better stop this, or I'll end up in tears. I'll have my lovely memories tucked away. It's time to look to the future."

With him, Nick thought. A future with him.

She pushed herself to her feet. "I've got to get busy. If I don't see you before, then we'll meet up for dinner."

"All right. I think I'll sit here a while."

Their eyes met for a long, quiet, special moment. Then Pippa smiled and walked away. Nick watched her until she disappeared from view.

"Oh, Pippa," he said, "we have forever magic. Please remember that."

The following two days passed much too quickly for Nick. He helped Pippa, as well as Emma, sort and pack. The little girl plowed through her possessions and decided she couldn't part with a thing.

Pippa made arrangements for some of their belongings to be shipped to Las Vegas, while the rest were to be held in Phoenix until she had a place to live. Nick kept silent as she called a realtor in Las Vegas and made an appointment to see rental properties when she arrived. She did not ask his advice on areas of town, and he didn't offer his opinion, although his teeth ached from his jaw's being clenched so tightly to keep him from speaking.

They made love at night in her bed, and then he would return to his own cabin to toss and turn until dawn, missing her. He did not like sneaking away in the dark like a thief. He wanted to kiss Pippa awake at dawn's light and make sweet, slow love to her before the busy day began. They'd agreed that Emma shouldn't see him in Pippa's bed in the morning, but he still didn't like having to dress and leave her. And he wasn't going to like it any better once Pippa got to Las Vegas.

On his last night at Serenity Cove, the Paulings joined them for dinner, and toasts were made to bright and happy futures. He received a hug from Grandma and a firm handshake from Grandpa. Pippa was to leave for Vegas as soon as the sale of Serenity Cove was completed, and she promised to call Nick before starting the drive. He tucked Emma into bed that night, telling her he'd be leaving in the morning before she got up.

"Have a wonderful birthday party, sweetheart," he said, "and I'll see you in Vegas very soon."

"I'll make my special wish when I blow out the candles on my cake."

"You do that. I like that wish. I love you, Emma."

"I love you, too, Nick. Bunches and bunches."

At dawn the next morning, Nick knocked lightly on Pippa's door. She flung it open and launched herself into his arms, kissing him passionately.

"I miss you," she said breathlessly.

"I haven't left yet."

"You're about to, and I miss you. I'll miss Peaches, too. Oh, this is awful."

"Then hurry yourself over to my world. Oh, Pippa, I love you so much. I'll be waiting for you. If you can finish up here any faster, do it. This is going to be agony. I'll call you tonight when I get there."

"All right. You'd better go before I start to cry. I love you, Nick Capoletti. Thank you for being so patient with me, with what I have to do once I get to Vegas."

"You promised you'd think about that."

"I will. I'll sort through everything that you and Grandma and Grandpa have said about my having already proven I can provide for myself and Emma. Right now, I can't see it. I still feel like a very protected child. Maybe things will become clearer to me once I've settled in over there."

"I hope so. I want to marry you yesterday, but you know that."

"I miss you."

"Oh, Lord."

He kissed her until neither of them could breathe, then turned and strode to his car. He drove away quickly, with Peaches nestled on the passenger seat, the image of Pippa standing on her porch waving good-bye vivid in his mind.

Tabor and Jared Loring listened intently as Nick spoke, and watched him pace back and forth across the living room of their suite at Miracles.

At last Nick stopped in front of the sofa where they were sitting and threw up his hands.

"That's it," he said. "That's the whole story."

Jared shook his head. "It's nuts, Nick. From what you've said, Pippa has already proven she can support herself and Emma. You two should be getting married the day Pippa gets here."

"Wrong," Tabor said.

"Thanks a helluva lot, Tabor," Nick muttered, dropping into a chair.

"All right, my love," Jared said to Tabor, "let's hear your womanly wisdom."

"First of all, Nick," she said, "I'm so happy you've

fallen in love. I can hardly wait to meet Pippa and Emma."

"Don't rush out to buy a dress for the wedding," Nick said gruffly. "Fashions will probably have changed by the time Pippa agrees to marry me."

"And that is nuts," Jared said.

"No, it isn't," Tabor said. "You're both seeing this from a totally male point of view. All evidence states that Pippa is perfectly capable of taking care of herself and Emma, so Nick is ready to jump in and be the protector, take on his role as Pippa's husband."

"Right," Nick said. "That's exactly right."

"That's exactly wrong, Mr. Capoletti, because Pippa doesn't yet realize how far she's come and how much she's grown. She has to discover that on her own so that she has a sense of inner peace. She's wise enough to know that. You'll just have to be patient and wait."

"I'm hating this," Nick said. "I am really hating this."

"I don't blame you, buddy," Jared said. "Life would be so much simpler if women weren't so complex."

"We have to be complex in order to understand men," Tabor said, combing her hand through Jared's silver hair. "Nick, you told Pippa that you understood what she needs to do."

"Yes, but then I got an even clearer picture of what I suspected to be true. Tabor, Pippa doesn't have a damn thing to prove to anyone."

"Only to herself," Tabor said. "Don't fight her on this, Nick, or you'll end up the loser. Be your wonderful, charming Italian self, and above all, be patient."

"I'm beginning to hate that *word* too," he said. "I'm in love, for crying out loud. I want to get on with my life with Pippa. I want to be a husband, and a father to Emma and Ben."

"Who's Ben?" Tabor asked.

"Oh, well, he comes later. He's the baby brother Emma wants."

Jared laughed. "You sure plan ahead."

"I know what I want, Jared," Nick said quietly, "and I've waited a long time for this. I can't lose Pippa. I won't."

Jared leaned forward and rested his elbows on his knees, lacing his fingers loosely together. "Nick, let me tell you something. I envy you for having recognized love the moment it hit you. Everyone around me knew I was in love with Tabor before I did. I was just a confused mess, walking through the day biting everyone's head off."

Nick chuckled. "Believe me, I remember."

"It was Tabor who had the wisdom," Jared went on. "She waited me out, then confronted me with her emotions, forcing me to recognize my own. What I'm saying is that women are wonderful, warm, giving creatures. And wise. A lot has happened very quickly to Pippa. Give her a chance to settle down and settle in. Give that womanly wisdom a chance to surface and set things to rights. They're amazing, these women we love. Don't screw this up by storming the gates of her mind in typical dumb, macho male fashion. What she's doing might not make sense to you and me right now, but the bottom line is, Pippa is a woman in love, and that makes her smarter than you and me put together."

"Oh, Jared," Tabor said, smiling at him warmly. "I can't believe you said all that."

He leaned back. "Every word of it is true."

"Oh, " Nick said. "Well . . . Oh." He got to his feet. "I think I'll go talk this all over with Peaches. Thanks for hearing my tale of woe. I appreciate your friendship, time, and advice. I'll see you later." He left the suite.

Tabor wrapped her arms around Jared's neck. "You're a wise and wonderful man, Jared Loring. I hope everything works out for Nick and Pippa."

"I think it will if Nick doesn't run out of that word he's starting to hate. Patience."

"I want them to be as happy as we are. Everyone should be as happy as we are."

Jared pulled her close. "Sounds good to me, Mrs. Loring, but all we can do for Nick now is be here if he needs us. He's at that heaven-and-hell stage in his relationship with Pippa."

"And you, Mr. Loring?"

"Tabor, my love," he said, "I'm in one-hundred-percent heaven."

He covered her mouth with his, and there was no more talking in the Loring suite for a long, long time.

Pippa lay in bed staring up into the darkness, unable to sleep. She felt in limbo, hovering between a vague here and there. Nick had called her that evening when he'd arrived in Las Vegas, and he'd seemed so far away. She missed him dreadfully, and already ached to see him again.

Still, the thought of leaving Serenity Cove and the life she'd known there saddened her, as did saying good-bye to the Paulings. A door was closing on an entire chapter of her life, a door that would never be opened again. That was the here, measured now in hours until its end.

And the there? It was waiting for her in Las Vegas, but was a gray, foggy blur. A job, a place to live, were just words with no form or substance, unknown entities. Only Nick was clear in her mental picture of her new life.

Only Nick. But she couldn't, wouldn't rely on him because he was there. She had to stand on her own two feet, prove to herself what she so desperately needed to know.

Pippa sighed. Her purpose was clear in the light of day. But in the darkness, as she lay alone in her big bed, tired from her tedious daily chores, she missed Nick Capoletti. She wanted him there with her, right then. She loved him with all she was, but the sad truth was that until she did what she had to do, all she was, wasn't enough.

Was it?

No, no, it wasn't, not yet.

But Nick had said that what she'd done over the years at Serenity Cove proved that she—

No.

Even the Paulings agreed with Nick and—

No.

"Oh, Pippa, stop it," she said, pressing her hands to her aching temples. "You know you're right about this. You know you are."

Wasn't she?

Eight

The following ten days were a study in frustration for Nick. He kept busy, telling himself it was the only hope he had of hanging on to his sanity. He was thoroughly convinced that he was going slowly but surely out of his mind.

He and Jared had agreed on a division of duties that would allow them both to work days the majority of the time. For the time being, however, Nick stayed on the night shift, somehow finding it easier to sleep during the day. His attempts to sleep at night had resulted in nothing but long hours of restlessness. He thought of Pippa constantly, no matter what the hour, and missed her more than he was able to express in words, even to Peaches. There was an empty ache within him, a hollowness that he knew only Pippa could fill. He spoke to her every night on the telephone, but it wasn't enough. Nothing but holding her in his arms would make him feel complete.

Dressed in his custom-tailored tuxedo, he strolled

through Miracles just after midnight, the day before Pippa's arrival. The gaming floor was crowded and noisy, the level of excitement and anticipation high.

He gazed around the room, trying to imagine how it would look to Pippa when she saw it for the first time. Would she find it gaudy and overdone? He hoped not. To him it was elegant, decorated in good taste. There was an aura of class to Miracles, and Jared's pride and joy, the sweeping carpeted staircase from the Scarlett and Rhett era, added a special, whimsical touch.

Nick shook his head and walked on. He had no idea what Pippa's reaction to Miracles would be. Nor did he know how long it would take for her to figure out that she was a competent, independent woman, and agree to marry him. He didn't know the number of lonely nights he would be sentenced to while Pippa lived somewhere else.

Damn, he thought. He was tired of this. He felt like a marionette whose strings were being pulled by forces over which he had no control. His restlessness, frustration, and loneliness were churning within him.

"Mr. Capoletti?"

He jerked his head around, focusing on the cocktail waitress standing beside him. "Hello, Nadine. What's wrong?"

Nadine frowned. "There's a man at blackjack table three who's had too much to drink. He's insisting I bring him another drink, but I know I shouldn't. The dealer signaled me to get help to have the guy moved out of there."

"I'll take care of him," Nick said. "Table three?"

"Yes. He's big. Sloppy and fat, but big. He's wearing a Hawaiian print shirt and is becoming very obnoxious. Believe me, you can't miss him once you get to that area."

"Okay, you stay clear for a few minutes." He patted her on the arm. "It's your stunning good looks, Nadine. You draw these wonderful guys like flies."

She rolled her eyes and walked away.

Nick strode toward the end of the room and caught the attention of a huge man standing by the wall, dressed in a tuxedo. Nick jerked his head, and the man came quickly to his side.

"Pico," Nick said, "we've got a loud drunk at table three, blackjack. I'll see what I can do on my own. You stay in the background, and let's hope we don't cause a scene."

"I'll be there, and I'll be ready to move in."

"Okay. Let's go."

As Nick approached the table he saw in an instant that neither Nadine nor the dealer had overreacted to the situation. The man was roaring his displeasure over the cards dealt him, and demanding that he be served another drink. The other players at the table were hastily collecting their chips and moving away. The drunk man was huge, had to be six feet five, and easily weighed three hundred pounds.

"A bone-cruncher," Nick muttered. "I don't need this hassle." He slid onto the chair next to the man. "Take a break, Rob," he said to the dealer.

"Yes, sir." Rob walked away.

"Hey!" the man yelled. "Where in the hell you goin', punk? I want cards here. I want a drink, too. Where's that little girl with the drinks?"

"She's busy," Nick said quietly, "and this table is closed. What's your name, buddy?"

"Who wants to know?" the man asked, glaring at Nick.

"I'm Nick Capoletti, and I'm going to decide if you

can have more cards and another drink, so I suggest you be nice to me. What's your name?"

"Jake Willingham from Idaho, that's who I am, and don't you forget it. I'm an important man where I come from."

"I'm sure you are," Nick said, "and important men have to protect their reputations. You don't want word to get back to Idaho that you had too much to drink and caused a scene while you were in Vegas, do you? Why don't you come with me and we'll find some coffee?"

"Buzz off, sonny," Jake said, poking Nick in the chest with one fat finger. "You can't tell me what to do."

Nick sighed. "Yes, Jake, I can, and I am telling you. Now, we can leave the floor quietly or put on a real show for these folks. It's up to you."

"I'm not going nowhere with you, kid. Cards!" he roared. "And where the hell is my drink?"

Nick stood and clamped Jake's shoulder with his hand. "That's it for tonight, Jake."

"You've got three seconds to get your hand off me, sonny boy," Jake said, snarling, "or I'm going to take you apart."

A murmur started in the crowd that had stopped playing to watch the two men. Nick knew the rules. Get the drunk off the floor and things back to normal as quickly as possible, with a minimum of force. Jake, however, had obviously not read the rule book.

"Jake, there are other people here from Idaho," Nick said, his hand still firmly in place. "They'll tell the folks back home about this. You don't want that to happen, do you? Of course not. Let's take a little walk."

"I'm not moving, penguin suit," Jake said, "so you can just forget it. Get your hand off me."

"All right."

Nick turned his head slightly to nod to Pico. The instant he looked away from Jake, the big man pulled back his arm and delivered a stunning blow to Nick's right eye. A collective gasp of alarm was heard from the watching throng as Nick toppled backward and landed heavily on the floor. Pico stepped in, hauled Jake out of the chair, and gave him a quick pop on the jaw with a closed fist. Jake crumpled to the floor like a sack of potatoes. A cheer went up from the crowd, and four more big men in tuxedos gathered around Nick and Jake.

"Take him to the small office," Pico said. "Sober him up, and hold him until you get further word."

"Come on, fatso," one of the men said. "The party's over."

Pico dropped to one knee beside Nick, who was still spread-eagled on the floor. He slapped Nick lightly on one cheek.

Nick moaned as he opened his eyes. He struggled to sit up, and was hauled to his feet by Pico. He staggered slightly, then gently probed his aching eye. "That Idaho potato sucker-punched me."

Pico chuckled. "He got in a good one, all right. At least he didn't break your pretty nose."

"Oh, thanks. Why doesn't that make me feel any better? Let's get off the floor. Enough is enough."

He started walking unsteadily away, with Pico right by his side. A round of applause went up from the audience, and he waved a hand breezily, trying to give the impression that it was all in a day's work.

"I'm dying," he said under his breath, one hand covering his throbbing eye. "Tell Pippa that I love her, but I died before she got here."

Pico laughed, but quickly quieted when Nick managed to glare at him with his good eye.

A small man in his forties, wearing a white waiter's jacket, rushed up to the pair. "Holy smokes, Nick, I heard there was a ruckus out here. Looks like you got slam-dunked."

"Well, hell, Trig," Nick said, "the guy was six eight and weighed four hundred pounds. What do you want from me?"

Trig peered at him. "Four hundred pounds? Four?"

Pico held up three fingers.

"I saw that, Pico," Nick said. "I may have only one eye, but I saw that. Trig, bring an ice pack up to my suite, will you?"

"Right away."

"And get Jerry to cover the floor, so I can die in peace."

Trig laughed as he headed toward the kitchen.

"I can get upstairs on my own, Pico," Nick said when he and Pico reached the private elevator to the suites. "Have the cops come pick up Potato Jake and let him sleep it off in the tank. Tell them Miracles isn't pressing charges."

"Okay, but are you sure you're steady enough on your feet? The potato really decked you, Nick."

"Yeah, I'm all right. Death cures all. Oh, Lord, how am I going to explain this to Pippa? I'm going to be a swollen raccoon when she gets here."

"Women like to fuss over guys. She'll love it."

"No, she'll hate it, because I told her Miracles was a classy place, and I had a nice, calm, nonthreatening job, just as any other man."

"Oh. Well, this doesn't happen too often, you know. You usually charm the socks off the drunks."

"My charm was worth zip tonight, that's for sure. Jared is going to laugh himself silly."

"Yep. You'll hear about this one for a while."

"Go away. You're making me more depressed than I already am." Pico started off, chuckling softly. "And the potato weighed four hundred, Pico," Nick called after him. Pico gave him a thumbs-up sign without breaking stride. "Well, three-fifty, maybe," Nick mumbled.

A short time later, Nick was sprawled in a chair in his living room with an ice pack pressed to his eye.

"It's gonna be a beaut of a shiner," Trig said.

"Pippa arrives tomorrow."

"Uh-oh."

"Tell me about it," Nick said glumly.

Trig shook his head. "From what you said when we all had dinner together the other night, Pippa is a real fine lady, Nick. Her kid sounds like a dandy little gal, too. We were talking after you left, you know, saying how great it was that you'd found someone special, the way the boss had. Jared and Tabor are really something together. Anyway, we all agreed that we'd be on our best behavior when Pippa first came, so she'd like us and Miracles straight off."

"I appreciate that, Trigger."

"Yeah, well, you screwed it up, Nick. You're going to look like a beat-up thug from the streets when she gets here. Then you gotta tell her you got creamed right here at Miracles. Why didn't you duck?"

"He sucker-punched me, Trig," Nick yelled. "I never saw it coming. Oh, my eye, my head, my face." He pulled the ice pack away. "Is the swelling going down? Is it turning color yet?"

Trig closed his eyes and shook his head. "Don't ask. That is one ugly mug you're flashing there. Put that pack back on."

"My face is frozen."

"Well, your brain isn't. You'd better start thinking of a reasonable explanation for your Technicolor face to give to Pippa."

"There isn't a reasonable explanation. Well, there is, but not one that will go over terrifically with her. This will cement her idea about casinos, which is none too flattering. Damn, why did this have to happen now?"

"Well, what's done is done," Trig said. "I'd better get back to work. You gonna be all right here alone? You're not dizzy or anything, are you?"

"No, I'm fine," Nick said sullenly. "I'll just sit here and turn my face into an iceberg. Thanks for your help, Trig."

"Sure thing. Page me if you need anything else."

"Yeah, okay."

"See ya."

As the door closed behind Trig, Nick pulled the ice pack away and gingerly examined his face.

"What a disaster," he muttered. His glance fell on the violet sitting on the coffee table. "Can you believe this, Peaches? Can you honest-to-heaven believe the lousy timing of this? Oh, I'm dying."

Late the next afternoon, Pippa and Emma arrived at their motel in Las Vegas. While Emma watched television, Pippa took a soothing shower to relieve her fatigue and the ache in her muscles from the long, tedious drive. She dressed in a yellow cotton sundress that was amazingly unwrinkled after being packed in the suitcase, then stared at her reflection in the mirror.

"You're in Las Vegas," she said. "You're actually here, and so is Nick."

Nick, she thought, smiling. He was only minutes away, instead of hundreds of miles. Oh, how she'd missed him. Hearing his voice on the phone every night had only made the ache of loneliness worse, the need to see him more intense. At last she would be with him.

She left the bathroom and was greeted by the noise of a blaring television. She crossed the room and turned the volume down.

"Mommy, I can't hear it," Emma said.

"The whole city can hear it." She picked up her watch and glanced at it before fastening it on her wrist. "Nick will be here in ten minutes to take us to dinner. You'd better put your shoes on."

" 'Kay," Emma said, sliding off the bed. "Can we have a TV in our new house? We never had one at Serenity Cove. I love to watch TV."

"There was no television reception that high up, Emma. We'll get a small television, I guess."

"Super. I like it here. I like this motel, too. I never been in one of these. Can we live in this place?"

Pippa laughed. "No, this is just for short stays. We'll only be here until we find a nice little place to live." She paused. "I'm beginning to realize how many things you've never experienced before. Well, that's all going to change now. Once we get settled, I'm going to take you to museums and the library, and we'll go on all kinds of wonderful outings that you'll enjoy."

There was a knock at the door.

"Nick," Pippa whispered. The speed of her heartbeat seemed to triple.

"Oh, boy, oh, boy, it's Nick," Emma said. "Can I open the door?"

"No. Remember what I said? You don't open the door

in a big city unless you're sure you know who it is."
She went to the door. "Who is it, please?"

"Nick."

Nick, Nick, Nick, she thought happily. She slid the
safety chain off and opened the door. "Nick, I'm so
glad—Oh, my Lord. Nick!"

He raised his hands in a gesture of peace as he
stepped into the room. "Now, don't get excited. I can
explain." He opened his arms to her. "Ah, Pippa, come
here."

She went eagerly, wrapping her arms around his
waist as he held her tightly. His lips sought hers, and
she welcomed them, savoring his taste, taking the heat
from his body into her own.

Oh, how she'd needed this, she mused dreamily.
She'd missed him so much, and loved him so very, very
much.

"Wow," Emma said, awed.

Nick's head snapped up. "Emma." He glanced at the
little girl, then smiled at Pippa. "Hold that thought."
He reluctantly released Pippa and grinned down at
Emma. "Nope, you're not Emma. She was a tiny thing,
only five years old. You're big, really big. You look six,
like someone who's ready for first grade. Okay, kid,
what did you do with my Emma? I want to give her a
hug, so get her out here."

Emma giggled in delight. "It's me. I'm Emma. I'm
six. My birthday party was super, and I really like my
crayons you got me."

"Are you sure you're Emma?"

"Yes, yes, I'm Emma."

He swung her up into his arms. "Then give me a
hug. I missed you, kiddo, I really did."

Emma threw her arms around his neck and hugged

him so tightly, he yelled for mercy. She released her hold and frowned.

"How come your eye looks funny?" she asked. "It's not even open much, and it's purple and blue. How come?"

"Yes," Pippa said pleasantly, "how come?"

Nick set Emma back on her feet, then straightened. "My eye. Yes, well, a person would wonder about that, wouldn't she? I certainly would if someone I knew showed up with a black eye." He paused. "My, you ladies look lovely in your pretty dresses. I'm glad I wore a tie and jacket, since I'm going to have two gorgeous dates. Ready to go eat?"

"Nick, your eye," Pippa said. "Could we back up to 'how come'?"

Damn, Nick thought. "Okay, here it is. There was a big guy at the casino who was really sloshed, and—"

"Sloshed?" Emma said, cocking her head to one side.

"He had too much to drink," Pippa said. "Not soda pop, but liquor. We've talked about that, Emma."

"Oh, yeah," she said, nodding. "You're not supposed to drink too much of that stuff."

"Right," Nick said. "Well, this man did drink too much, and he wasn't behaving very nicely, so I asked him to please come with me and have some coffee."

"Were you charming?" Pippa asked politely.

"I was oozing Italian charm," he said, feeling a trickle of sweat run down his back, "but he wasn't buying it. So, well, he sort of took his best shot and popped me in the eye."

"Wow," Emma said. "That was naughty of him. Did it hurt?"

He shrugged. "Not much. But do understand that this doesn't happen all the time at Miracles. My charm usually does the trick just lickety-split. This was a rare occasion, not the norm at all."

Pippa's hands flew to her mouth, and she backed up. Sinking onto the edge of one of the double beds, she bent over slightly, her shoulders shaking.

"Oh Lord, she's crying," Nick said. He hurried over to her and dropped to one knee beside her. "Pippa, please don't. I swear this doesn't happen all the time. I was furious about the whole thing, because I knew you'd be upset. Pippa, the casino isn't filled with drunks ready to start a fight. I swear on Peaches' blossoms that it isn't like that. Pippa?"

"Are you sad, Mommy?" Emma asked peering over Nick's shoulder. "Please don't be sad. The naughty man was bad. Nick wasn't bad. Mommy?"

Pippa straightened and dropped her hands. "This is hysterical." She laughed, wrapping her arms around her stomach as the merry resonance bounced through the air.

Nick's eyes widened, and he got slowly to his feet. "You're not crying? You're laughing?" He planted his hands on his hips. "And what, pray tell, do you find so amusing about all of this?"

She gasped for breath, then nodded. "There. I'm finished. Oh, my, that's funny." She stood up and placed her fingertips gently on Nick's swollen cheek. "You poor baby. That must hurt like the dickens."

"I'm waiting, Pippa," he said gruffly. "Why is this funny?"

"Because I know you're worried about my reaction to Miracles, and you must have been a nervous wreck about having to explain all this to me. It's not funny that you were hurt, but the timing is so terrible, it's hysterical. Nick, your career is your choice to make, and I was acting like a child when I pitched a fit about it. I accept what you do for a living, black eye and all."

He looked up at the ceiling for a long moment. "Praise the Lord." He smiled at her. "This has been the worst day of my life. I didn't know how I was going to explain this to you. It really isn't a common occurrence, Pippa, I swear it."

"I believe you," she said.

"I'm hungry," Emma said, apparently deciding the subject of Nick's eye was becoming boring.

"Then let's go eat," Nick said. "I'll be the envy of every guy in the restaurant." He draped his arm around Pippa's shoulders as Emma opened the door. "Thank you, Pippa," he said quietly, "for being so understanding. I love you so much, and I'm very glad you're finally here."

"I love you too," she whispered.

"Are you coming?" Emma called from the corridor.

"Yes, we're coming," Nick said. He looked quickly around the room. "Two beds, but one room. Why do I get the feeling I'm destined to take another cold shower tonight?"

"I'll have my own place soon," Pippa said.

He nodded, and they left the room.

Her own place, he thought as they walked to his car. Hers. He could visit, spend the evening, make love to her, then drag on his clothes and return to his empty bed at Miracles. He'd be kept just outside the circle of her life, waiting until he had permission to enter. This was all so wrong, so damn wrong!

"Nick?" Pippa asked as he opened the car door for her. "Are you all right? You suddenly seem tense. Is your eye bothering you?"

"What? Oh, no, it doesn't hurt much. I'm fine, just hungry."

"Me too," Emma said.

The restaurant that Nick had selected catered to families. There was a special children's menu, and Emma was given a frilly paper apron to wear. The food was delicious, and Emma recounted every detail of her birthday party for Nick.

Pippa was hardly aware of what she ate as Nick's proximity to her in the circular booth caused desire to swirl unchecked through her. His thigh pressed against hers with increasing frequency, but when she looked at him, his attention was riveted either on his meal or on Emma.

He knew what he was doing under that table, Pippa thought, taking a bite of shrimp. Did he think he was the only one who'd suffered from their days and nights apart? And just then, he was driving her crazy, the bum.

She daintily dabbed her lips with her napkin, then replaced the napkin in her lap with exacting care and smiled sweetly at Emma. Then she slid her hand onto Nick's thigh, her fingers drawing lazy circles on the taut muscles.

Nick stiffened, and nearly choked on a sip of water. He shot a quick look at Pippa, but her attention was on Emma. He cleared his throat roughly, but Pippa's fingers continued their tormenting, tantalizing foray over his thigh.

Nick stifled a noise that was a mixture of a groan and a chuckle. Oh, she was something, his Pippa. She knew darn well that his pressing his leg against hers was no accident, and she was paying him back in spades. She was driving him up the wall, that was what she was doing. How long could he bear the agony and ecstasy of her busy little fingers?

"Cut it out," he muttered out of the side of his mouth.

She batted her eyelashes at him. "Pardon me?"

"No," he said, laughing, "I won't pardon you. You're wicked." He reached under the table, gripped her hand, and firmly placed it back in her lap.

"Tit for tat, Mr. Capoletti," she said, smiling. "I missed you, too, you know."

"Don't start talking about it. Things are, shall we say, hard enough."

She burst into laughter, he scowled, and Emma looked at them in total confusion.

Their waitress appeared at the table. "Excuse me, but there's a magician about to perform for the children. Your daughter can come sit by the stage if she'd like to watch the show, and you'll be able to see her clearly from here."

"Well, daughter?" Nick said to Emma. "What do you think?"

"Oh, yes," Emma said, clapping her hands. "I want to. Can I, Mommy?"

"Sure," Pippa said.

Emma slid out of the booth and walked with the waitress to the low stage on the far side of the restaurant.

"Alone at last," Nick said. "Take off your clothes and we'll make whoopee on the tabletop."

"Okay," Pippa said. "Sounds good to me."

Nick took her hands and gazed seriously at her. "This is crazy, Pippa. It's as if you're here, but you're not. I'm going to ache for you tonight, just as I have every night since I left Serenity Cove. Please don't misunderstand me. I love Emma, you know I do; it's just that . . . Never mind. There's no way to say this without it sounding as though I resent Emma's being in that room with you tonight instead of me. I don't resent

Emma. It's the whole way our relationship is set up that's getting to me. No, forget that too. This isn't the time or the place to go into it."

Pippa squeezed his hands. "I know you don't resent Emma, Nick. I'm her mother, and I wish she weren't going to be in that room tonight. Maybe that sounds terrible, but it's true. I love you, I've missed you, and I want to make love with you very, very much."

He laughed. "That's it. Get up on the table."

"Don't tempt me. I think we'd better change the subject. The Paulings send their love to you. They're in Phoenix, staying at a motel while they're house-shopping in the retirement community."

"I hope they'll like their new life."

"I'm sure they will. They're very excited about it."

"And you, Pippa? Are you excited about your new life?"

"What do you mean?"

"Just what I said. You're about to become an independent woman. You'll be living in your own house, working at a job of your choice, managing your own money, time, social life. You'll be making all the decisions."

She frowned. "Nick, what is it? There's an edge to your voice, as if you're—I don't know—angry."

Oh, damn, he was blowing it, Nick thought in self-disgust. His anger was closer to the surface than he'd realized, mingled with a sense of helpless frustration. This wasn't fair to Pippa, and he had to get himself under control. She had come there under the impression that he understood what she felt she needed to do. But what about her promise to consider that she might have already accomplished all she thought she had to? Not tonight, Capoletti, he told himself. Lighten up.

"Nick?"

"Hey, I'm sorry." He kissed her gently on the temple. "I'm just tired. This dumb eye was throbbing like a toothache all last night, and I didn't get much sleep. You've got to be exhausted yourself, after that drive."

"Yes," she said, still frowning slightly, "I'm very weary."

"We'll make an early night of it. As soon as Emma is finished watching the show, I'll take you back to your motel. What's on your agenda for tomorrow?"

"I'm meeting a realtor at nine. I want to find a place to live first. Something close to a good school, a school that has arrangements for transportation with a day-care center. The woman I talked to at the real-estate office said that's a common arrangement, since most mothers work these days."

Nick nodded.

"Emma is going to have a lot of adjustments to make, but she's so eager to have other children to play with that I'm hoping she'll do well."

"I'm sure she will," he said, managing a smile. "Then you'll look for a job?"

"Yes, once we have a place to live, I'll start checking the want ads."

"Do you know what kind of work you'd like to do?"

"No. I did a little bit of a lot of things at Serenity Cove, but I don't feel I have expertise in anything."

"That's not true, Pippa. You have bookkeeping skills, you could be a reservations clerk, you have experience in advertising. The list is endless."

"I check leaky roofs rather well," she said, smiling.

"Take that one off your list."

"Well, one step at a time. First up is a place to live. A furnished place. Even with my lovely nest egg the Paulings gave me, I don't want to spend a bundle on furniture. I don't know how long it will take me to get a job or how much I'll be earning. I'll have to watch my pennies until I get a clear picture of where I stand."

And where in the hell did *he* stand in all of this? Nick inwardly raged. Everything Pippa was saying was in the singular, and her constant use of "I" was grating his nerves raw. Where she should be standing was right next to him, as his wife! He had to get out of that restaurant before he blew a fuse and ruined everything.

"Nick, are you sure nothing is wrong?" she asked. "You seem to have switched moods very quickly."

"I'm fine. Listen, call me at the casino tomorrow when you're free."

"Yes, all right. I really have no idea how long this is going to take. I just hope this woman has found some nice places for me to look at." Pippa fiddled with her napkin. She was suddenly wishing that Nick was coming with her to inspect the houses and apartments. He had experience in these things, and she had absolutely no idea what she was doing.

But it was even more than that, she knew. She wanted to see Nick in the different places, see if they suited him as much as they did her and Emma. They would be spending a lot of time together, the three of them, and Nick had the right to feel comfortable in her home.

No, no, Pippa told herself quickly, that was wrong. She was supposed to be doing this independently, separate and apart from Nick Capoletti. But how did she separate her thoughts from the man she loved? He was an intricate, vitally important part of her life. She felt splintered, pulled in two. Her mind was trudging down a road of independence, while her heart was tugging in the opposite direction, toward Nick.

She was tired, Pippa reasoned, totally exhausted as

the long day caught up with her. Her confusion would be swept away by a refreshing night's sleep. She'd be fine in the morning, her purpose clear. Yes, she'd be just fine.

Squeals of delight and the sound of applause came from the group of children across the room. Pippa looked up to see a man in a top hat and cape take a deep bow, then disappear behind a curtain. A few moments later, Emma came running back to the table, her green eyes sparkling with excitement.

"Oh, he was super," she said. "He had a white bird in his hat that wasn't there when we looked inside, and his handkerchief was a paper flower when he snapped his fingers. He gots magic!"

Nick smiled at Emma, then signaled to the waitress. He gots magic, he thought. Nick Capoletti and Pippa Pauling had magic, too, of a totally different kind. The problem was, he was beginning to wonder if Pippa remembered that.

Emma chattered about the magician during the ride back to the motel. Nick and Pippa commented in all the right places, but they were lost in their own thoughts. As soon as the door to their room was open, Emma made a beeline for the television, though Pippa stayed out in the corridor with Nick. She gazed up at him, but couldn't read the expression on his face. However, she could see a muscle jerking in his jaw.

"Thank you for a lovely evening," she said, then shook her head. "What an inane thing to say. I'd rather tell you again how much I've missed you, how much I want to make love with you tonight."

He chuckled softly. "The 'lovely evening' bit is easier on the libido, but the other is nice to hear. I'd better get out of here. Call me tomorrow."

"Yes."

He lowered his head and brushed his lips over hers. In the next instant, he pulled her close to him, his mouth possessing hers in a demanding kiss. She molded herself to him, relishing the feel of him. Desire exploded within her. This was Nick, and this was now. They were together again after so many long, lonely days and nights. This was Nick, the man she loved. And she wanted him.

"Good night," he said when he finally lifted his head. "Sleep well. I love you, Pippa. Remember that, okay?"

Before she could draw enough air into her lungs to speak, he turned and strode away. She watched him go, then entered the room, closing the door behind her with a quiet click, shutting out everyone beyond it.

Nick drove for an hour through the desert before returning to Miracles. Darkness had fallen, and the bright lights of the casinos lit up the area as though it were day. As he was driving he'd made his mind a blank, thinking of nothing, allowing no emotions to surface. When he entered Miracles, he felt totally drained and strangely hollow.

Jared crossed the gaming floor to meet him. "So?" he asked. "How'd it go? How's Pippa? Emma?"

"Fine," Nick said, attempting a smile that failed.

"What about your eye?"

"No problem. She's accepted my career, has it all squared away in her mind."

"Hey, that's terrific, Nick," Jared said, smiling. "That must be a relief."

"Yeah."

"You're back early, aren't you?"

"Well, Pippa was tired. She had a long drive. We went to dinner and . . . They had a magician for the kids. Emma loved the show." Nick laughed, a sharp, humorless bark of sound. "Yep, little Emma now believes in magic."

Jared frowned. "Nick, what—"

"Listen, Jared, I'll go change and take over the floor. I can sleep tomorrow, because Pippa's going to be busy. I'll be back down in a bit." He walked away.

Trig appeared at Jared's side. "Nick looks like he just came from a funeral, instead of from seeing his lady, boss. She flip out over his eye?"

"No. Nick says that Pippa is all settled down about Miracles."

"Well, that's good," Trig said. "Then why does Nick look like death warmed over?"

"I don't know, Trig," Jared said, running one hand across the back of his neck. "But something is wrong. Something is very definitely wrong."

Nine

Pippa stood alone in the small living room, her arms wrapped around her waist as she once more scrutinized the area.

It was a darling house, she told herself. Made of red brick, and with two bedrooms, the house was at the end of a quiet cul-de-sac and was perfect for her and Emma. The furniture was nothing fancy, but was sturdy and comfortable. They were only three blocks from an elementary school, and another block from a day-care center that cooperated with the school. Pippa couldn't have hoped to find a better location.

"Yes, perfect," she said decisively, then felt the ache of unshed tears in her throat.

What on earth was the matter with her? she wondered in disgust. By eleven o'clock that morning the house had been hers on a month-to-month rental basis. The realtor had made some phone calls, and Pippa now had the utilities in working order. The phone company would install a telephone the next day. She and Emma had checked out of the motel and already unpacked their sheets, towels, and enough kitchen supplies so that Pippa could cook dinner. They'd shopped for groceries, and Pippa had called with the address for the moving company in Phoenix, left a message for the Paulings at their motel, and talked briefly with Nick, giving him directions to the house. At that very moment, Emma was playing next door with an eight-year-old girl named Leanne.

"Perfect," Pippa said again, then sniffled. It was a cute house, she told herself. This was a nice neighborhood, the school was close . . . But it all felt so strange, and she didn't want to be there!

Maybe, she thought frantically, once the rest of their belongings arrived it would feel more like their home, instead of just a house where they'd stopped off for a while. The books, knickknacks, pictures, and the rest of their clothes would add the needed familiar touches.

Tears slid down her cheeks as she glanced around again. She didn't want to sit on that sofa, or cook in the kitchen, or take a shower in the pretty pink-and-white bathroom. She was acting ridiculously, she admonished herself. She should have been counting her lucky stars that she'd found such a nice place so quickly. Emma was bubbling with excitement; so happy, she was glowing.

"But what about me?" Pippa asked aloud, sprawling onto the sofa. She dashed the tears from her cheeks and took a deep, wobbly breath.

Why had she been so close to crying for the past hour? she asked herself. Why was she so depressed, a gloomy, dark cloud seemed to be hovering over her head? Why wasn't she exhilarated about this first step in her quest for independence, in her goal to prove she could provide for herself and Emma?

She'd done it all alone, and should have been proud of herself.

Alone.

She was lonely.

Something was missing.

Nick Capoletti.

Pippa looked deep within herself and reviewed all that she had done at Serenity Cove since arriving there when Emma was six months old. She'd worked hard. She'd juggled her chores around the tending of her baby, had maintained a home, and provided Emma with a stable life.

What she'd come to Las Vegas to prove to herself she could do, she'd already done for more than five years!

"Oh, Lord," she muttered, pressing her hands to her cheeks. *That* was why she felt no surge of excitement about her new house. This was a rerun, something she'd done before. There was now no doubt in her mind that she could find a job to her liking, a job for which she would be well qualified. Everything was falling into place with exacting order and a minimum of fuss.

But she was lonely.

She was, she understood at long last, a complete, independent, competent woman, entirely capable of providing for herself and Emma.

And she was a woman in love.

She was ready to move forward and take her place at Nick's side as his wife, his partner for all time.

"Well, dandy," she said, frowning as she folded her arms over her breasts. She'd messed up this situation royally. There she sat, with a few days to wait for her remaining possessions to arrive so she could unpack them and get settled into a house she didn't even want to be living in. Her stubbornness, her refusal to listen to what Nick and the Paulings had been telling her, had gotten her into this muddle. She would have liked to paddle her own bottom for being such a dunce, for being so out of touch with the woman within herself.

"Hi, Nick," she said aloud. "Like my house? Well, guess what? I made this teeny-tiny error in figuring out who I really am. So, I'm moving out of this place I moved into today, to live with you as your wife. Nifty, huh? Oh," she said with a moan. "He won't buy that for a minute."

And why should he? she reasoned. *She* could hardly believe the truths that were slamming against her brain. It would appear to Nick, and with just cause, that she'd panicked, lost her nerve once she realized she was on her own, and was leaping into his arms for protection.

"So, now what, Pippa dear?" she asked herself sarcastically. "How are you going to get yourself out of this predicament?" She didn't know, which did nothing to improve her increasing depression. To bare her soul to Nick now would sow seeds of doubt in his mind as to her motives. She wouldn't blame him one bit for questioning her sudden about-face. Cute little light bulbs supposedly only blinked on over the heads of cartoon characters. In reality, people usually worked through their confusion one step at a time, until the fog lifted and the answers were clear.

And that, Pippa thought dismally, was what she was going to have to *pretend* to do. She wouldn't run the risk of destroying her relationship with Nick by sowing those seeds of doubt in his mind. Doubt could choke and smother the beautiful, rare, special love she shared with Nick.

She detested the idea of playing out a charade, but she'd boxed herself into a corner with her stubbornness and her lack of confidence in herself. Better that *she* should pay the price for her actions than to dump those seeds of doubt onto Nick. They could destroy all that they had together.

How long, Pippa wondered, would she have to play out her less-than-honest role? Good heavens, how should she know? She'd never done anything so blatantly deceitful in her life. This was definitely not her cup of tea, but she had no choice. She'd have to say and do things over a period of time that would convince Nick she'd reached the proper decision, as a sane person would have. She could only hope she would see her way clear to telling him the truth soon. The very thought of her deception was making her head ache. Putting it into action would probably give her an ulcer.

As Nick drove through the gathering dusk, he was oblivious to the glorious, vibrant sunset streaking across the desert sky. His mind was divided between maneuvering through the heavy traffic and working on his attitude.

He had his act together, he told himself. Ever since Pippa had called to tell him where she was living, he'd been rehearsing bright, cheerful enthusiasm.

He'd really blown it the previous night, he admonished himself. Pippa had noticed his sudden mood switch, and he'd barely managed to bluff his way through with lame excuses. Well, no more of that. He'd told Pippa she'd have the time she needed to prove herself, and she'd have it. Even if it was totally ridiculous. Completely unnecessary. Absurd. Driving him straight up the wall.

"Shape up, Capoletti," he muttered.

Emma had told him that tantrums didn't cut it with Pippa. Getting her to promise to think about her impressive work record at Serenity Cove apparently hadn't gotten him anywhere either. She was charging full steam ahead with her plan. If he pushed her, she'd dig in her pretty little heels, and he would gain nothing. So, now he would be gung ho, Mr. Charming Italian of the Year. He'd gush and smile and tell Pippa that everything she was doing was awesome. He wasn't crazy about his new plan, but it was the best he could come up with.

He checked the street signs and turned right, then left, then right again, weaving his way through a quiet, well-kept neighborhood made up of small brick houses. As he approached the end of the cul-de-sac, looking at house numbers as he went, he spotted Emma sitting on the front porch of the last house. She jumped up and waved when she saw him.

Nick smiled. Lord, he loved that little girl. She was going to grow up to be a beauty, just like her mother, and he wanted to be there as her father every step of the way. He'd hear her laughter, see her smiles, dry her tears. He'd do his part in getting Emma a baby brother named Ben, and love Pippa, heart, mind, body, and soul, until the day he died. If Pippa ever agreed to marry him.

"Enthusiasm, Capoletti," he said, pulling into the driveway. He was smiling as he got out of the car.

"Hey, Emma," he called. "How are you?"

She ran to meet him, and he swung her up into his

arms. After setting her back on her feet, he turned to survey the house.

"Say, now," he said, "that is one fine house you've got there, ma'am."

"My friend Leanne lives right there," Emma said, pointing to the house next door. "She's eight, but she goes to the school I'm going to go to."

"Super. Let's go inside, and you can give me a tour. What's your mom doing?"

"Looking in the paper for a job. She said she got to get a job real quick."

"Mmm," he said, practicing his smile again.

When Nick entered the living room with Emma, Pippa put down the newspaper and crossed the room to him. He kissed her deeply, stopping only when Emma broke the spell with an exuberant "Wow!"

"Well, well, this is dandy," he said, looking around. "Cute as a button. Yes, sir, just the right size for the two of you. You and Emma will be snug as bugs here, Pippa. What more could you want?"

You! Pippa screamed silently.

"Come on, Nick," Emma said, grabbing his hand. "I'll show you my room. My stuff isn't here yet, but my room will be great when all my toys are in there."

"Lead on, Miss Emma."

A few minutes later, Nick returned to the living room alone, still smiling.

"I've got to hand it to you, Pippa," he said, not looking directly at her, "you did good. I think you and Emma will be very comfortable here." He rapped on one wall with his knuckles. "Sturdy, seems well insulated. It gets chilly here in the winter, but you should be toasty-warm."

Winter? Pippa thought. It had been a hundred and

seven degrees that afternoon. Winter had to be months away. Wasn't he going to tack on something that would at least hint that he hoped they'd be married by then? No? Why not?

"I . . . um, I think I'll feel more settled after our belongings arrive," she said, gazing intently at him. He was peering at the carpeting as though it were the most fascinating thing he'd ever seen. "I'll have a phone tomorrow."

"Oh, that's good. We'll be able to keep in touch more easily."

"Keep in touch?" she repeated, her eyes widening.

"Yeah, you know, chat on the phone. You ask me how my day was, I ask you how your day was, stuff like that." He paused. "So, what's the scoop in the want ads? Anything strike your fancy? Are you ready to pound the pavement? There's always a big turnover in the casinos, but I'm not familiar with the general business-type jobs. It must be pretty exciting to be on the brink of a new career. I know I was hyped when I came to Miracles. I bet you're raring to go. Right?" He smiled his best hundred-watt dazzler.

"Right," Pippa said, managing a very weak smile. "There's a bookkeeping job in a dentist's office, and a position for a convention coordinator at one of the big hotels."

"You could do either one of those."

"Yes, well, I have to check the locations on my map, because it wouldn't be wise to get something too far from here. Emma will have a long enough day as it is. I don't want to be tied up in traffic for an extra hour, getting home."

"I swear, Pippa, you think of everything." Except him. Except that she could work part-time if she wanted to after she married him, and be home for Emma when school got out. They could get a bigger house, with lots of bedrooms for more children. But Pippa's mind was obviously traveling down an entirely different road than his, and she was scaring him to death. "Listen, how about driving over and taking a look at Miracles?"

"Now?" she asked, glancing down at her jeans and green knit top.

"I'm not dressed up either. Emma can't go on the gaming floor, but there's a side corridor where we can stand, so you both can see everything. Then I'll take you up to my suite and show you where Peaches lives. Okay?"

"Yes, all right. I'll go tell Emma. Make yourself comfortable."

"Hey, how could I not be comfortable in this great little place? Yep, it really suits you and Emma. It's the perfect size for two lovely, delicate ladies."

"Right," Pippa said miserably, and hurried from the room.

Nick puffed out his cheeks and released a pent-up breath. His enthusiasm was nauseating, he thought, phony as a three-dollar bill, but Pippa was buying it. Wasn't she? She seemed rather subdued, but she'd had a big day and was probably tired. They'd go to Miracles and relax in his suite. Then he'd bring them home, and when Emma was all tucked in and asleep, they'd . . . No, he'd better not dwell on that. His libido was off the Richter scale as it was.

He glanced around the living room once more. It *was* a cute house, but Pippa didn't belong there. She should have been out with him, looking for a big home where all of them could live. So far, he was pulling off his enthusiasm routine, but the knot in his gut told him it was costing him. Oh, Lord, he hated this!

Pippa stood with Nick and Emma in the side corridor at Miracles and stared out at the floor of the casino. It wasn't until her chest began to ache that she realized she was hardly breathing.

"It's beautiful," she said. "It's absolutely beautiful."

Nick put his arm around her and kissed her on the temple. "I'm very glad you like it."

"Oh, I do."

"I betcha Cinderella came down those stairs," Emma said. "Did she, Nick? Was Cinderella here?"

"Well, I didn't see her if she was," Nick said, "but I imagine that anyone who came down those stairs would feel like Cinderella. Tabor walked down them once with Jared. She was wearing a red dress, and everyone was watching her. You'll have to ask her if she felt like Cinderella."

"Or Scarlett O'Hara," Pippa said. "Tabor and Jared are so nice, Nick. I felt comfortable with them the moment we met. And I liked Trig, Spider, Mrs. Tuttle, Pico. . . ."

Nick laughed. "The whole group. Yeah, they're good people, good friends. They've all been eager to meet my two special ladies ever since I got back from Serenity Cove. Well, why don't we go upstairs to my suite and say hello to Peaches? Who's interested in having some ice cream sent up?"

"Me," Pippa and Emma said in unison.

"Then let's do it."

Across the room, Trig was standing beside Jared and

Tabor. "Well, boss," he said, "Pippa and Emma are great, don't you think?"

Jared nodded. "Yes, absolutely. But . . ." His voice trailed off.

"But?" Trig prompted.

"Nick is uptight. Things are not as idyllic as they appear."

"I agree," Tabor said. "There's a current of tension between Pippa and Nick. It's subtle, below the surface, but it's definitely there, like a lull before the storm."

"Some storms don't amount to much," Jared said.

"I know, my love," Tabor said, "but others destroy everything in their path."

Late that night, Pippa lay with her head on Nick's chest, lazily tracing a circle on his chest with one fingertip. Their lovemaking had been urgent, almost rough, as the flames of pent-up passion consumed them. In a pounding rhythm, they'd sought and reached the summit of their ecstasy, then were flung over the edge. Now they were silent and content, needing nothing more then to be close to each other.

Pippa laughed softly.

"Hmm?" Nick murmured.

"How terrible would I be if I said, 'Thanks, I needed that'?"

"You're terrible."

"Okay. I really did have a lovely time at Miracles, Nick. I feel very foolish when I realize how wrong my preconceived ideas about casinos were. I'm sorry."

"No harm done. You gathered new facts and changed your opinion. That's what counts. A person could . . . Well, do that about a lot of things." Such as feeling she had to prove herself. "You have to be willing to stop and take inventory." When? When was she going to keep her promise, take stock of herself, and agree to marry him? "Get the drift?"

"Yes," Pippa said. She wanted to tell him then, right away, that she'd figured it all out, knew she was ready to become his wife. "I understand." But it was too soon, too risky.

"I guess I'd better get going," Nick said. No, dammit, he didn't want to leave. It shouldn't have been like that.

No! She didn't want him to go. "Yes, I suppose so."

He sighed as he left the bed. He pulled on his clothes, then bent over to kiss her.

"Good night, Pippa. I love you. I'll lock the door on my way out."

"I love you too. Oh, Nick, I—"

"Yes?"

"Nothing."

Nothing, he thought as he left the house. Nothing, he repeated, driving away. That was what he felt he had, standing outside the circle of warmth again. What good was love, what good was the forever magic, if it wasn't his to claim?

He pounded his fist on the steering wheel. He'd had it, he fumed. He'd be damned if he'd make love to the woman of his heart, then drag himself out of bed and sneak away in the darkness. And the hell with his phony enthusiasm, too. Pippa's house might have been cute, but she didn't belong there! She could go about proving herself to her heart's content, but he'd be damned if he'd play the role of the obedient, back-burner lover anymore. He'd had enough.

He stopped at a red light. "You might lose her,

Capoletti," he mumbled. He ran a shaking hand down his face. Lose Pippa? Emma? Dammit, no. But he didn't want to go on like this.

How could Pippa? Didn't she love him as much as he loved her? What if she figured out she was perfectly capable of providing for herself and Emma and liked it that way, enjoyed her independence so much that he would be relegated to a thief-in-the-night lover for all time? "No!" he said, hitting the steering wheel again.

He'd watch and listen carefully for a little while longer, he decided. He'd pay close attention to what Pippa said and did, and determine which road she was choosing for herself. Just a little while longer.

"Pippa? It's Nick. I got your message."

"I'm so glad you called. Nick, I got the job in the dentist's office. Isn't that wonderful?" It smelled in the dentist's office, she thought glumly. She'd always hated the way dentists' offices smelled. "I start tomorrow. Emma will go to the day-care center all day until school starts."

"Well, congratulations. You sound very pleased." She was getting everything she wanted, he thought. Didn't she want *him?* "Things are really coming together for you."

No, they weren't! "Yes, they certainly are. Can you come over tonight?"

"I . . . um, no, I have floor duty. Jerry has the flu. Look, I've got to go. I'll talk to you tomorrow. Good luck on your first day on the job. 'Bye."

" 'Bye," Pippa said to the dial tone, and slowly hung up.

• • • •

"Pippa, this is Nick. Hey, I'm sorry I haven't called, but the flu really hit the staff here. We're shorthanded, and I'm filling in all over the place. How's the job?"

"Fine," she said. Awful. She could hear the drill in her little office. All day long she heard that God-awful drill and smelled that smell. "Dandy. Super," she added brightly. "I have four days under my belt." Four gruesome days. "I miss you, Nick. I wish you could come over, at least for a few hours. It's only nine o'clock now."

A few hours? That was it? The hell he would. "No can do, Pippa. Is Emma ready to start school tomorrow?"

"Yes, she's very excited. She's been asking where you are."

"Well, you'll have to explain it to her. Yeah, Pippa, you do that. Explain to Emma why I'm not there."

"Nick? What is it? You sound angry."

"And you sound as though everything is going exactly the way you want it. I bet you have a nifty schedule all worked out for you and Emma."

"Well, yes, but it's necessary. It's difficult to work all day and keep up with the chores around here. If I didn't have a schedule it would be a disaster. There doesn't seem to be a spare minute to squeeze in one more thing."

"I see," Nick said quietly. "Well, that's clear enough."

"What do you mean?"

"I'm being paged, Pippa. I'll—I'll see ya."

Nick turned from the telephone in the side corridor off the floor and found himself staring at a scowling Tabor.

"Hi," he said. "How's life?"

"I'm sorry I eavesdropped on your conversation. . . .No, forget that. I'm not sorry at all. What's this malarkey about the staff's having the flu? There's no flu epidemic at Miracles, Nick Capoletti. And you weren't paged, either. Talk to me, Nick. Why are you dusting Pippa off? Why the lies? I thought you were in love with her, wanted to marry her."

"I am. I do," he said loudly. "But she doesn't need me for a damn thing. She said it herself. She's scheduled to the hilt with her challenging new job and spiffy little house. She doesn't have, quote, 'a spare minute to squeeze in one more thing.' Guess what, Tabor? I'm not on the schedule. Oh, sure, she'd give me a few hours here and there, but that isn't enough, not for me. She's proving to herself what she was so determined to prove, and she's loving it. I waited as long as I could, Tabor. I listened and watched, but Pippa doesn't have room for me in her life. I'm out of patience and out of charm. It's over. Finished."

"Oh, Nick, no. Go to her, talk to her."

"What's the point? I'll only hear what I already know."

"Nick, it can't end like this, with lies over the phone. You owe it to yourself and Pippa to see her. Please, do that much. If you're calling it quits, at least do it with a little class."

"Class?"

Tabor folded her arms across her chest. "Yes Capoletti, class. I'm so-o-o disappointed to think you'd end a relationship over the phone, with lies about flu epidemics. So-o-o disappointed."

"You are?"

"I am."

"Well, hell."

"Go to her, Nicholas."

"All right, fine," he said gruffly. "I don't know what

difference it makes, but I'll go. When something is over, it's over, Tabor."

"Nick . . ."

"I'm going!" He strode away.

"Very clever, my sweet," Jared said, appearing from around the corner.

"Oh, Jared, I don't know whether it was or not. He's so hurt, so disillusioned, but I really believe he needs to see Pippa, talk to her. Things aren't always the way they seem, you know."

"Ah, that womanly wisdom again."

"I just want Nick and Pippa to be happy, to have what we have. What happens tonight is going to determine their entire futures."

"You're right," Jared said, frowning. "Terrific. Now I'm going to be a nervous wreck while we're waiting for Nick to come back."

"Come with me, Mr. Loring," she said, smiling at him. "I know just what to do to calm your jangled nerves."

It was nearly ten-thirty when Nick pulled into Pippa's driveway. He folded his arms over the top of the steering wheel and stared at the small house. Lights glowed behind the closed drapes in the living room.

This was it, he thought gloomily. The end. He'd driven around for a while, postponing this confrontation, but Tabor was right. After what he'd shared with Pippa, loving her as much as he did, he needed to say in person what had to be said. He'd have his heart shattered with a little class. Hell.

He got out of the car and shook his head. Talk about class, he thought wryly. It wasn't every guy who came for the last time to see the woman he loved, decked out in a tuxedo.

His steps dragging, Nick crossed the lawn, to the front door. His heart was thudding painfully, and he resisted the urge to cut and run. Before he could change his mind, he knocked on the door.

"Who is it, please?"

"Nick."

The door was flung open. "Nick," Pippa said, "what are you . . . ? Oh, my goodness, you look beautiful."

His gaze swept over her, taking in her baggy shirt, cut-off jeans, the shadows beneath her eyes, and the mop she held in one hand. Hello, my Pippa, he thought. Hello, my love. Good-bye, my love.

"What's the mop for?" he asked, stepping into the house. "Is that your weapon of defense when someone comes to your door late at night?"

"I was washing the kitchen floor," she said, as she closed the door. Why was he there? He hadn't smiled, hadn't touched her. . . . "I'm surprised to see you."

"Washing the floor? At this hour?"

"I have to do some chores late. There just isn't time earlier."

"Then rearrange your damn schedule," he yelled. "You're exhausted, I can tell."

"Shh. You'll wake Emma."

"I'm sorry," he said, lowering his voice. "Pippa, could you put the mop away? I realize this visit wasn't pen- ciled into your schedule, but I'd like to talk to you."

"Why are you harping about my schedule?" she asked, narrowing her eyes.

"Because I'm not on it! That's why I'm here, Pippa, to tell you that I can't do this anymore. I tried, I swear to God, I tried to be patient long enough for you to prove to yourself what you needed to know. But it's all falling apart, don't you see that? I didn't have much patience in the first place, because what you were doing was so unnecessary. And now you've set up your routine, your damnable schedule, and you're perking right along . . . without me. You don't need me, Pippa. Maybe you still love me, but your focus is on yourself, on the world you're creating for you and Emma. There's no room for me, for us, except for when we go to bed together. Then I pull on my clothes and disappear into the night because I'm not part of your morning routine. I can't, I won't, live like this." He took a shuddering breath. "It's over, Pippa. Finished."

A rushing noise roared in Pippa's ears, and black dots danced before her eyes. She blinked, clearing her vision as she tightened her hold on the mop.

"Over," she repeated, then cleared her throat when she heard the quivering in her voice. "Finished. Because you doubt my need for you in my life? Seeds of doubt, and they were nurtured, weren't they? Nurtured by my excitement over this house, my job, the fact that I'd settled myself and Emma into a routine. Is that right, Nick? Did all those things nurture those seeds of doubt?"

He dragged one hand through his hair. "Yes, if you want to phrase it like that. I call them cold, hard facts. You promised me you'd stop long enough to really look at all you did during those years at Serenity Cove. You didn't keep that promise, Pippa. You just plowed ahead, and I kept getting pushed further and further out of the circle. Our love was magic, forever magic, but you're not making room for it in your life. I—" He stopped, his voice too choked with emotion. "I've got to go. Tell

Emma . . . Tell Emma I'm sorry about Ben." He turned and opened the door.

"If you go out that door," Pippa said, "I'll slug you with this mop."

He glanced back at her. "What?"

"You heard me. You've had your say, and I deserve mine."

"Why? So you can repeat everything I already know? Forget it."

"I'm warning you, Capoletti. I'm going to bean you with this thing if you don't listen to me."

He closed the door and leaned back against it, folding his arms across his chest. "So speak, but make it snappy. I've got some serious drinking to do."

"How very macho of you."

"That's enough," he said, and pushed himself away from the door.

Pippa dropped the mop and raised her hands. "Wait. Please. Nick, I . . . Nick, I . . . Nick, I . . ."

"Pippa!"

"Lied!"

"What?"

"That's what I did, all right. I lied. Oh, Nick, on the day I moved in here I knew I'd made a mistake. I kept my promise to you, and I realized as I thought about those years at Serenity Cove that I didn't need to prove anything to myself. I'm a complete woman, and a woman in love. I knew I was ready to be your wife, your partner."

Nick straightened, dropping his arms and curling his hands into tight fists. "Why in the hell didn't you tell me?"

"I didn't think you'd believe me! I was so afraid you'd decide I'd simply lost my nerve about doing this on my own. I was afraid there would be seeds of doubt in your mind, nurtured by my lousy timing, my total about-face. So I lied. I was pretending to be ecstatic over this house, my job, so it would look as if I'd proven what I needed to over a reasonable period of time. Oh, Nick, this house is so empty without you. I hate my job, because it smells funny. I'm lonely and miserable, and I love and miss you. I thought I was doing the right thing, but the seeds of doubt were planted, anyway." Tears filled her eyes. "I'm so sorry. I hurt you, and I hate knowing that I hurt you. I thought I was doing the right thing." The tears spilled onto her cheeks. "But I was doing the wrong thing, and—Oh, God, say something."

"Your job *smells* funny?"

"Oh," she moaned, covering her face with her hands.

"Pippa." He pulled her hands free and gazed into her tear-filled eyes. "You put yourself through all this to protect our love? Our forever magic? What we have was that important to you, that special?"

"Oh, yes. I love you so much. I couldn't bear the thought of your possibly doubting me or my love for you. I should have realized that lies are never the answer, but . . . I'm sorry, Nick. If I could turn back the clock, I'd do it all differently, but I can't. I love you, I want you, and I need you very much."

Nick stared up at the ceiling for a moment in an attempt to regain control of his emotions. He gave up the battle and looked at her again, tears shimmering in his own eyes. "What you did, you did out of love, and I cherish that. There was no flu epidemic at Miracles, so I lied to you too. We're starting over fresh right now. Pippa, I love you. Will you please marry me? Will you be my wife, my life, my other half, my partner? Will you allow me to be Emma's father, and create Ben Capoletti with you? Will you be, until death parts us, my forever magic?"

"Oh, yes," she said, nearly choking on a sob. "Yes."

He kissed her. It was a gentle kiss, a soft kiss of commitment. It was a kiss that scattered the seeds of doubts into oblivion, and cast a glow of warmth over them together. It was a kiss that kindled their passions.

"I want to make love to you," Nick murmured, his voice husky with desire.

"Yes."

"Just one other thing."

"Yes?"

"Would you really have whopped me with that mop?"

She smiled up at him, love shining in her eyes. "Yes."

"That's what I thought." He chuckled. "You can quit your smelly job and be a bouncer at Miracles."

"Okay. Nick, according to my schedule it's time for you to make love with me now."

"We're going to discuss that schedule of yours, my organized wonder, but this is one instance when it's right on the money. I do love you, Pippa."

"And I love you, Nick."

With their arms around each other they walked into the bedroom.

And made love.

And it was magic. . . .

THE EDITOR'S CORNER

I am delighted to let you know that from now on one new LOVESWEPT each month will be simultaneously published in hardcover under the Doubleday imprint. The first LOVESWEPT in hardcover is **LONG TIME COMING**, by Sandra Brown, which you read—and we hope, loved—this month. Who better to start this new venture than the author of the very first LOVESWEPT, **HEAVEN'S PRICE**? We know that most of you like to keep your numbered paperback LOVESWEPTs in complete sets, but we thought many might also want to collect these beautifully bound hardcover editions. And, at only $12.95, a real bargain, they make fabulous gifts, not only at this holiday season but also for birthdays, Mother's Day, and other special occasions. Perhaps through these classy hardcover editions you will introduce some of your friends to the pleasures of reading LOVESWEPTs. When you ask your bookseller for the hardcover, please remember that the imprint is Doubleday.

Next month's simultaneously published hardcover and paperback is a very special treat from Fayrene Preston, the beginning of the trilogy *The Pearls of Sharah*. In these three LOVESWEPTs, a string of ancient, priceless pearls moves from person to person, exerting a profound effect on the life of each. The trilogy opens with **ALEXANDRA'S STORY**, LOVESWEPT #306 (no number, of course, on the hardcover edition). When Alexandra Sheldon turned to meet Damon Barand, she felt as if she'd waited her whole life for him. Damon—enigmatic, mysterious, an arms dealer operating just barely on the right side of the law—was the dark side of the moon beckoning Alex into the black satin night of his soul. But was it the woman he was drawn to? Or the impossibly beautiful and extravagantly valuable pearls she wore draped on her sensual body? This fascinating question answered, you'll be eager, we believe, for the two *Pearls of Sharah* romances to follow: in April, **RAINE'S STORY;** in June,

(continued)

LEAH'S STORY. You can count on the fact that all three books are breathlessly exciting reads!

Get ready for an offering from Judy Gill that's as poignant as it is playful, LOVESWEPT #307, **LIGHT ANOTHER CANDLE.** Sandy is rebuilding her life, at last doing the landscaping work she loves, when Richard Gearing comes bumping into her life. For Rick it is love at first sight; for Sandy it is torment from first encounter. Both had suffered terribly in their first marriages, and both are afraid of commitment. It takes her twin daughters, his young son, and a near tragedy to get these two gorgeous people together in one of the best surprise endings you'll ever hope to see in a love story.

Here comes one of the most original and thrilling romances we've published—**NEVER LET GO**, LOVESWEPT #308, by Deborah Smith. We're going to return to that super couple in **HOLD ON TIGHT**, Dinah and Rucker McClure. Their blissful life together has gone sadly awry—Dinah has disappeared and Rucker has been searching for her ceaselessly for almost a year. He finds her as the book opens, and it is a hellish reunion. Trust shattered, but still deeply in love with Dinah, Rucker is pulled into a dangerous, heart-wrenching chase for the woman he loves. Filled with passion and humor and surprises, this story of love regained is as unique as it is wonderful.

Please give a *big* welcome to a brand-new author, Lynne Marie Bryant, making her publishing debut with the utterly charming **CALYPSO'S COWBOY**, LOVESWEPT #309. When Smokejumper Caly Robbins parachuted onto the wilderness ranch, she expected to fight a fire—not to be swept into the arms of one thoroughly masculine, absolutely gorgeous black-haired cowboy. Jeff Adams was a goner the minute he set eyes on the red-haired, petite, and feisty lady. But her independence and his need to cherish and protect put them almost completely at odds . . . except when he was teaching her the sweet mysteries of love. A rich, vibrant love story from an author who writes authentically about ranchers 'cause she is one!

(continued)

Helen Mittermeyer follows up her thrilling **ABLAZE** with another hot romance next month, **BLUE FLAME,** LOVESWEPT #310, in which we get Dev Abrams's love story. Dev thinks he's hallucinating when he meets the shocked eyes of the only woman he has ever loved, the wife who supposedly died a few years before. Felicity, too, is stunned, for Dev had been reported killed in the middle of a revolution. But still burning brightly is the blue flame of their almost savage desire for each other, of their deep love. In a passionate and action-filled story, Dev and Felicity fight fiercely to reclaim their love. A must read!

Patt Bucheister gives us one of her best ever in **NEAR THE EDGE,** LOVESWEPT #311, the suspenseful tale of two people who were meant for each other. Alex Tanner had agreed to guard the daughter of a powerful man when fate made her the pawn in her brother's risky gambit. But the passion whipping between him and Joanna Kerr made it almost impossible for him to do his job. Set in Patt's native land, England, this is a very special novel, close to the author's heart . . . and, we suspect, one that will grow close to your heart, too.

Altogether a spectacular month ahead of great LOVE-SWEPT reading.

Warm good wishes,

Carolyn Nichols

Carolyn Nichols
  Editor
LOVESWEPT
Bantam Books
666 Fifth Avenue
New York, NY 10103

THE DELANEY DYNASTY

Men and women whose loves and passions are so glorious it takes many great romance novels by three bestselling authors to tell their tempestuous stories.

THE SHAMROCK TRINITY

THE DELANEYS OF KILLAROO

Now Available!
THE DELANEYS: *The Untamed Years*

Special Offer
Buy a Bantam Book
for only 50¢.

Now you can have Bantam's catalog filled with hundreds of titles plus take advantage of our unique and exciting bonus book offer. A special offer which gives you the opportunity to purchase a Bantam book for only 50¢. Here's how!

By ordering any five books at the regular price per order, you can also choose any other single book listed (up to a $5.95 value) for just 50¢. Some restrictions do apply, but for further details why not send for Bantam's catalog of titles today!

Just send us your name and address and we will send you a catalog!